What O
about

"R.J. Patterson does a fantastic job at keeping you engaged and interested. I look forward to more from this talented author."

- Aaron Patterson
bestselling author of SWEET DREAMS

DEAD SHOT

"Small town life in southern Idaho might seem quaint and idyllic to some. But when local newspaper reporter Cal Murphy begins to uncover a series of strange deaths that are linked to a sticky spider web of deception, the lid on the peaceful town is blown wide open. Told with all the energy and bravado of an old pro, first-timer R.J. Patterson hits one out of the park his first time at bat with *Dead Shot*. It's that good."

- Vincent Zandri
bestselling author of THE REMAINS

"You can tell R.J. knows what it's like to live in the newspaper world, but with *Dead Shot*, he's proven that he also can write one heck of a murder mystery."

- Josh Katzowitz
NFL writer for CBSSports.com
& author of Sid Gillman: Father of the Passing Game

"Patterson has a mean streak about a mile wide and puts his two main characters through quite a horrible ride, which makes for good reading."

- Richard D., reader

DEAD LINE

"This book kept me on the edge of my seat the whole time. I didn't really want to put it down. R.J. Patterson has hooked me. I'll be back for more."

- Bob Behler
3-time Idaho broadcaster of the year
and play-by-play voice for Boise State football

"Like a John Grisham novel, from the very start I was pulled right into the story and couldn't put the book down. It was as if I personally knew and cared about what happened to each of the main characters. Every chapter ended with so much excitement and suspense I had to continue to read until I learned how it ended, even though it kept me up until 3:00 A.M.

- Ray F., reader

DEAD IN THE WATER

"In Dead in the Water, R.J. Patterson accurately captures the action-packed saga of a what could be a real-life college football scandal. The sordid details will leave readers flipping through the pages as fast as a hurry-up offense."

- Mark Schlabach,
ESPN college sports columnist and
co-author of *Called to Coach*
and *Heisman: The Man Behind the Trophy*

THE WARREN OMISSIONS

"What can be more fascinating than a super high concept novel that reopens the conspiracy behind the JFK assassination while the threat of a global world war rests in the balance? With his new novel, *The Warren Omissions*, former journalist turned bestselling author R.J. Patterson proves he just might be the next worthy successor to Vince Flynn."

- Vincent Zandri
bestselling author of THE REMAINS

INTO THE

SHADOWS

A Brady Hawk novel

R.J.
PATTERSON

Into the Shadows
© Copyright 2018 R.J. Patterson

First Print Edition 2018

Cover Design by Books Covered

Published in the United States of America
Green E-Books
Boise Idaho 83713

For Blake, a true gentleman
and an even greater man

CHAPTER 1

The Al Hajar Mountains, Oman

BRADY HAWK ADJUSTED THE STRAPS on his backpack and then glanced over his shoulder at the Australian couple lagging behind him. The man fumbled with his water bottle, while the woman stopped to take another picture of a goat herder guiding his flock toward a pasture with more vegetation. With the sun arching high above them, Hawk figured this was as good of a time as any to stop and eat lunch.

"You guys hungry?" Hawk asked.

"I thought you said there was a great place to eat near a waterfall," the man said, a scowl rippling across his forehead.

"We can press on," Hawk said. "It's your dime. I just thought because you both keep stopping to rest so often, it might be good to put something in your bellies so we can finish the hike."

The man, who went by the name of Liam

Turner, glared at Hawk.

"What exactly are you suggesting?" Turner asked.

The woman, Lily, shot Liam a sideways glance.

"Do you have to take everything everyone says as some kind of slight toward you?" she asked, continuing on without waiting for a response. "You do this all the time when we're at home. I make one little comment and you would think that I just insulted your entire ancestry for the last thousand years. Just get a grip. Are you hungry or not?"

Hawk tried to hide his smirk. Lily's fiery response reminded him of Alex, whom he hadn't seen in almost nine months when he thought it was prudent to disappear. In a second, he was whisked away to a memory of when Alex stood up to one of the feistier foes they encountered while in Somalia. Engrossed in his recollection of the event, Hawk had let his guard down and was grinning ear to ear.

"Hey, asshole," Liam said as he stormed toward Hawk. "You think that's funny?"

Hawk snapped back to reality just in time to avoid Liam's right hook. Acting on instinct, Hawk ducked before going low and putting Liam on his back. Hawk was about to pummel the snarky Aussie's face before thinking better of it. Instead, Hawk hopped up and offered his hand to Liam.

Swatting dismissively at Hawk, Liam climbed to

his feet unassisted.

"Is that how you treat all of your clients?" Liam asked with a snarl.

"Only the ones who try to throw a punch at me," Hawk said. "Now, I'll ask again. Would you like to eat here or wait until we reach the waterfall two hours from now?"

"I think I'm ready to go back," Liam said.

"I'm starving, Liam," Lily said as she stuffed her camera back into her bag. "Let's eat now."

"No, I want to go back right now. If we stopped, this jarhead would get to eat as well. He doesn't deserve a break after what he did to me."

She shook her head. "Liam, you were the one who was about to—"

"Save it, Lily. Let's get going, *Mr. Smith*," Liam said as he sneered at Hawk.

Hawk spun toward his two clients and walked back down the trail. Serving as a trail guide for Al Hajar Outfitters seemed like a good cover several months ago when Hawk needed to find a way to prevent the drain on his resources. If he had gone much longer without a job, he calculated he'd be destitute by the end of the year. But he also needed to go somewhere that not even Michaels would think to look. Hawk decided to go somewhere he never anticipated going himself. And the mountain region in Oman struck him as an ideal location to hide.

For the past few months, Hawk had lived simply, staying in a communal home supplied by his employer. In his short time there, he'd seen several other guides come and go—some warded off by the physical demand of climbing Al Hajar's steep and rocky trails, others by the oppressive restraints that go with living in a predominantly Muslim culture. Alcohol, if one could find it, was rare. Speaking openly and critically of the government could land you in jail. But mostly, the comforts of home were what people missed most—familiar food, television they could understand, music they appreciated, friends they loved.

Hawk longed for all those things, but he recognized the reality of his situation: if he ever wanted to go home in the future, laying low was imperative. The most powerful man in the free world had placed Hawk at the top of a list nobody wanted to be on. And he knew there was only one way people got off that list. But Hawk hadn't given up yet. Trudging up and down Al Hajar had given him plenty of time to think about another approach, one that could get his name erased from such a list without getting personally rubbed out.

"Would you mind slowing down?" Liam said. "You military people think you have to prove to everyone else just how tough you are."

Hawk stopped and turned around. He strode toward Liam before halting less than a meter away.

"You seem to have a problem with the military," Hawk said. "What makes you think I was ever in anybody's military?"

Liam huffed through his nose. "Are you kidding me? It's obvious. You've got Marine written all over you."

"Is that so?" Hawk said with a sarcastic smile. He wanted to put the snarky punk in his place but resisted.

"Yeah, the way you talk, the way you march, the way you think you're the boss of me instead of realizing that *I'm* the one paying your salary."

Hawk chuckled. "Guess I'm not gonna get a tip today, am I?"

"I'll give you a tip instead," Liam said. "Stop being such a hard ass and thoughtfully consider the people you're supposed to be leading. Not everyone cares to be treated like we're foot soldiers in your army. Not everyone—"

"That's enough," Hawk said.

"See, you're doing it right now," Liam said, putting his finger into Hawk's chest.

Hawk glanced down at Liam's index finger and then at Liam.

"If you don't remove your finger, I'm going to take you down again—and I promise you won't get up so easily this time."

"Is that so, Mr. Tough Guy?"

"Liam," Lily called, stamping her foot. "Cut it out."

Liam spun toward her. "If you speak to me like that again, you're going to regret it."

Hawk then grabbed a fistful of Liam's shirt and pulled him close.

"That's not how we treat ladies," Hawk said. "Now, I suggest you apologize to your lady."

Hawk released Liam, who stumbled a few steps down the path. When he regained his balance and stood upright, he glared up at Hawk.

"My patience has run out," Hawk said. "Now apologize and let's keep moving, or else I'm gonna leave you here."

Liam mumbled something to Lily before they resumed their hike, keeping pace with Hawk. They all walked in silence for the next hour. Hawk enjoyed the peace and quiet as well as the steady pace. Once they returned to the Al Hajar Outfitters office, Hawk took the couple into the back and introduced them to his boss so they could air their grievances.

"Did we have a problem today?" Abdul Majjeed asked the couple.

"It was great," Lily said with a smile. "Mr. Smith was a wonderful guide."

Majjeed turned to Liam. "I take it you didn't feel the same way."

Liam shook his head. "*Disaster* is a more appropriate way to describe today's hike."

"How so?" Majjeed asked, his eyebrows arched.

Hawk slipped out of the office and sat down on a chair in the hallway, listening to Liam's biased account of their interactions. According to Liam, he claimed he was assaulted by the military "goon" serving as their guide. He was ruthless and caustic—and unapologetically so, according to Liam.

Majjeed poked his head outside the office to find Hawk.

"Did you hear all of this?"

Hawk nodded.

"Is this true what this man is saying?" Majjeed asked.

"I don't know how you say it in Oman, but back home, we call people like him a 'prima donna,' someone who demands to get their way in all circumstances with no regard for others."

"That sounds like what he's accusing you of," Majjeed said.

"That's how they all do it."

Majjeed took a deep breath and nodded knowingly, as if he'd encountered such people before.

"Were you in the military?" Majjeed asked finally. "You never mentioned that to me before. That would've been important."

"Don't trust that fool," Hawk said. "He would've died on a marked trail if I hadn't helped him out."

"That's not answering my question."

Hawk shrugged. "I already answered it when I filled out my application to work for you. Besides, is it really that important?"

Majjeed returned to his office, but Hawk didn't move. He listened in on the entire follow-up conversation, which drove his next response.

Majjeed spoke in a hushed tone, but Hawk heard enough of the conversation.

"Did he really do these things to you?" Majjeed asked.

"Yes," the man answered, his head nodding furiously. "Every word of it's true."

"And you think he's ex-military?" Majjeed's voice softening again.

Liam nodded again. "No doubt about it."

Hawk didn't wait around to hear the rest. If Majjeed had an inkling of belief that Hawk was ex-military, there'd be an officer at his door to arrest him within an hour. He rushed home and crammed all his valuable items into a pillowcase, doubling as his suitcase. Without saying goodbye to even the closest of friends he'd made during his time at the outfitters, Hawk stole off toward the bus stop and caught the next bus headed for Muscat.

Hawk didn't look back either. Spending what felt like years of his life on the run gave him an odd comfort as he struck off for the big city. He needed a change of scenery, a fresh start, a place to hide. He needed a place to hatch his scheme for revenge on President Michaels.

* * *

HAWK SWALLOWED HARD when he heard the click of a gun from behind the door.

"Who is it?" the man on the other side asked.

"It's me, Brady."

"Hawk?"

"Yeah."

"Look up at the camera."

Hawk followed the instructions and flashed a toothy grin followed by a wave. But the door remained bolted shut.

"If it's really you, tell me what was my prized baseball card."

"That's easy, Ray—your Bo Jackson rookie. You even had it signed."

The deadbolt clicked before the door swung open. Instead of a joyful embrace, the man poked his head out into the hallway and glanced around before grabbing Hawk by his collar and yanking him inside.

Ray Green slammed the door behind him and secured the deadbolt before rearming the alarm system on the pad next to the door. He started to place the gun back into his shoulder holster before deciding to keep it out. He then gestured toward the living room with his weapon.

"Goodness, Ray, is Muscat that dangerous of a place?" Hawk asked. "This place looks like a fortress."

"I had two guards down there. What'd you do to them?"

Hawk raised his hands in a posture of surrender.

"Now, I know what this must look like to you, but I swear I'm on your side. I don't mean you any harm."

"It's been a few years, Hawk, and I haven't heard a word from you. Yet, you suddenly just show up on my doorstep, somehow eluding the two men patrolling the grounds."

"Come on. You know it couldn't have been that challenging for me. Besides, I didn't hurt them. Hell, they didn't even see me."

"What do you want?"

"I need your help."

"That's a pretty bold request, given what happened the last time I saw you. We needed your help that night too, but you went MIA on us."

"If you want an explanation, I can give it to you."

"Save it. Just tell me what you want so you can get on with it and get the hell out of my house."

Hawk eased onto the couch but remained hunched over, seated on the edge.

"I'm afraid my request isn't a small favor. I need your help to get back on my feet because I'm in a real bind."

"What kind of bind?"

"The kind of bind that being at the top of President Michaels' kill list will get you."

"What'd you do?"

"In short? Nothing—aside from saving his life. But I've also tried to expose his corruption, which is only me trying to uphold my oath to serve this country."

"Spare me the moral platitudes, Hawk. You lost that high ground when you abandoned us that night."

"Come on, Ray. We all make mistakes and—"

"Mistakes are leaving your meat on the grill too long. Leaving your brothers in the middle of battle? That's not a mistake. That is a conscious choice, a choice you made on your own."

"I don't know what else to tell you," Hawk said. "I probably should've never joined up when I did. I was going through a lot. I was young and foolish."

"And you're different now?"

Hawk nodded. "I know what I'm fighting for now. Besides, the Seals obviously weren't for you either. I mean, a private security contractor in Oman?

You're not exactly in a place to lecture me."

"I'd still be there if they hadn't forced me out."

"What'd you do?"

"I don't want to get into it," Ray said with a sigh. "Now, will you tell me what you're doing here?"

"To be blunt, I need a place to lay low—along with a job."

"With all his money, your dad can't find you something? Especially with all your experience—"

"He's not really my dad, but that's a story for another night. Even if he could get me a position with his company, I need one that keeps me off the radar. But Tom Colton has no idea what it means to go off the radar."

"What makes you think my boss will hire you? You don't even know him."

"Just ask him for me, will you? If you vouch for me, I'm sure he'd hire me."

"Like I said, you don't know Oliver Ackerman."

"Just help me out. You know I've got the skills and experience necessary, probably as good as, if not better than, most of his men."

"If I ask him, it's not going to be easy avoiding red flags. Getting hired to work in Oman requires working with the state department and the local government. There's plenty of vetting in that process."

"There doesn't have to be," Hawk said. "It'd just

be for a few months. Ask him to meet with me. That's all I want. He could just pay me under the table."

Ray exhaled slowly and shrugged. "Okay. I'll see what I can do in the morning. In the meantime, let me get you a blanket. You can sleep right there. It's late and I've got a big day in the morning."

"I really appreciate it, Ray."

Ray returned quickly with a pillow and a sheet for Hawk.

"The light's by that wall," Ray said. "You look tired. I'm going to bed now, and we'll catch up tomorrow."

"It's good to see you," Hawk said with a faint smile.

"You too. I just wish it was under different circumstances. Harboring you as a man on the lam isn't how I envisioned our reunion."

"Me either."

Hawk shuffled toward the bathroom and took care of business before heading back to bed. On his way to the couch, something on Ray's desk caught Hawk's eye. Hawk noticed a folder with a code name on it. He eased down the hall to make sure Ray's light was out. Satisfied that he had turned in for the night, Hawk eased back to the desk and rifled through the papers.

Hawk then stopped as his mouth fell agape.

I need to talk to Alex.

CHAPTER 2

Brighton, England

ALEX DUNCAN LOATHED MONDAYS for many reasons, reasons far beyond their simple existence on a calendar. Ultimately, they served as a stark reminder of the previous life she once had. She considered her job with Firestorm to be about as perfect as it could get, using her skills to shut down terrorists and keep Americans safe from rogue attacks. But today she stared at herself in the mirror as she combed her hair in an effort to look presentable before trudging off to her humdrum job.

When Hawk vanished, Alex and Blunt both decided they should do the same. Staying hidden in the U.S. was a difficult task given the amount of resources at President Michaels' disposal. So, they both headed to Europe—Blunt to the coast of Italy, while Alex went to England. Alex wasted little time in finding a job working for Lloyd's Bank in Brighton, a sleepy seaside town in the southern part of the country.

Using her hacking skills, Alex created an alternate identity for herself, complete with a healthy resume. However, she was careful to make sure that it didn't stand out so much that it seemed overly impressive to her prospective employers. Enough to get a job working for the company's cyber security division was her aim—and she succeeded.

In the months since the Firestorm team had parted ways, Alex struggled with the aftermath. The camaraderie she had experienced on a regular basis with Hawk trumped the mundane moments of sitting alone and pecking away on her keyboard. Yet now this was all she did with no respite. She shied away from developing any semblance of a social life given that she might have to disappear any moment and wouldn't want to leave behind any clues, much less deal with the burden of lying to everyone she met.

However, Alex found one silver lining in her new life—access. Working for Lloyd's gave her the ability to snoop without drawing much attention. She managed to hide her cyber footprint as she searched financial records and dug into the backgrounds of many aliases of terrorists and politicians alike. Although her work at Firestorm afforded Alex an array of resources, gathering the type of information that gave the team leverage over certain suspects also risked her exposure. One careless move and someone at NSA would have found great pleasure in turning her in to the agency's brass. But at Lloyd's, that precaution wasn't so necessary as long as she maneuvered carefully through the bank's system.

Working long hours and cyber snooping after hours, Alex compiled quite a treasure trove of useful information about some of Firestorm's biggest enemies as well as the biggest threats to America. However, she couldn't stop thinking about Hawk.

Before he disappeared, Hawk left Alex a note about a web-based account that he'd set up for the two of them. Instead of emailing messages back and forth to one another and risking the threat of capture, he suggested they communicate solely through writing drafts in the email account and leaving the messages unsent. By doing so, the messages would never be intercepted, allowing them to communicate as securely and discreetly as possible. The protocol was to erase the messages once the other person had read them.

Hawk had only sent two messages. The first one asked her if she'd heard anything about Shane Samuels' status. When Hawk decided to leave, Samuels was still in a coma. And as far as she knew, Samuels still was. His tenuous health situation gave her pause before deciding to leave the U.S. Blunt assured her that he'd take care of Samuels, getting him out of the hospital to somewhere safe before they left. But that promise went unfulfilled when Samuels was mysteriously moved elsewhere. She pressed the hospital for information about Samuels' transfer, but various nurses and supervisors denied her requests. Using her online sleuthing skills, Alex slipped into the hospital one night and asked one of the nurses for any details available on Samuels. She refused at first until Alex threatened to make public the married woman's affair with the hospital administrator. However, the only information available about Samuels appeared in a locked file that mentioned his transfer was a matter of national security. Despite her best attempts, Alex had failed to unearth any further news on him. He could've died or remained in a coma—or he could've been walking the streets healed and healthy. There was no way of finding out, she eventually concluded. Shedecided not to let Samuels' situation thwart her efforts to escape to Europe.

The second message Hawk sent pertained to where he planned to hide. Using a set of coordinates, he conveyed his location in the Al Hajar Mountains.

"Why would he go to Oman?" she wondered aloud when she figured out the meaning of his message before deleting it. "I guess it's as good of a hiding place as any."

Eight months had passed since she last read a message from Hawk, though that didn't deter her hope that she'd someday receive one.

Alex's daily morning routine consisted of grabbing a coffee at the corner bakery near her flat before visiting the library to check for a message from Hawk. She questioned her sanity for such a ritual. Starting each morning off with a dose of disappointment wasn't the best way to face the day, though she reasoned that the coffee offset any sunshine sapped up by the parade of frustration. The tradeoff wasn't necessarily a fair one, but she decided it'd have to suffice.

Mondays often seemed to be the most difficult to endure since they were the only day the bakery was closed.

"Caffeine-free disappointment, here I come," Alex muttered to herself as she trudged toward the library. Though she'd never asked the owners why, she had pondered away many hours in search of a possible reason for why the bakery closed on Mondays.

Of all days to deprive people of such a vital sustenance . . .

A light rain peppered the city as a thick fog rolled across the water toward land. She hoisted her umbrella and continued marching toward her destination.

Once she reached the top of the steps at the library, she lowered her canopy and shook off any excess water. Upon entering the facility, she headed straight to her preferred bank of computers and started her hammering away on the keypad. She logged into her library account using the legend Blunt helped her craft, one by the name of Sarah Roberts. A normal, unmemorable name designed to help her do one thing and do it well—blend in.

She then typed in her username and password for her joint email account with Hawk. In order to avoid suspicion, she sent out emails most days to various businesses, oftentimes with a fake resume attached. She rarely received anything beyond a standard reply, but she never anticipated having anyone seriously reply. But this Monday, things were different.

A bold number 1, bracketed by parentheses, grabbed her attention when she glanced at her inbox. She was so accustomed to seeing a bolded zero in that spot that she did a double take to make sure what she saw was real.

Let's see who's emailing me.

Alex furrowed her brow as she read the message. The sender's name was listed as John Doe, and he'd written a vague note, one that she couldn't readily interpret. She wondered if it was some sort of code or simply spam that had wormed its way into her inbox.

But nobody knows that this email address even exists.

She re-read the message again.

J'n dpnjoh gps zpv.

She shook her head as she studied the words once more. They still didn't make sense to her, and she wasn't immediately interested in cracking the code.

Instead of dwelling on it, she turned her attention to the draft folder, where she expected to see another empty slot. But a message with a header grabbed her attention.

"Re:URGENT" the title read.

Maybe I don't need coffee this Monday after all.

CHAPTER 3

Muscat, Oman

HAWK WAITED UNTIL RAY left for work before rousing from the living room sofa. The first beams of sunshine trickled across the floor as Hawk made his way to the desk where he'd discovered papers he surely wasn't meant to see. The conclusion was a logical one given that Ray had either taken the papers with him or locked them in one of the drawers. The only thing on the desk besides the keyboard and terminal was a sticky note giving Hawk instructions on how to log in to the computer as a guest.

Showing a similar distrust for Ray—and a penchant for exercising caution—Hawk carefully covered his cyber tracks as Alex had instructed him to do. He logged into their email account and composed a note for her, devoid of any salutations or extraneous words.

I wanted you to know that I've stumbled onto something big and I need your help. I had been planning a way to avenge our nemesis, but I've found something that just might be what we need to put him away for good. However, I can't do it alone. I need to infiltrate a private security company here, but I need a new legend, one that's rock solid online and completely believable. You've got one day to do it. Please respond either way to make it happen. If so, please send back a copy of my new resume for this venture as well as any other pertinent details about my new alias. I'll explain everything more in depth at a later time.

Hawk saved the message in the draft folder and closed out of the account. Using the tricks Alex had taught him, he erased all the folders and history that would've logged his visit to the email inbox on the computer. He closed the computer and leaned back in his chair. All he could do was wait for Ray to return home.

* * *

A FEW MINUTES before 6:30 p.m., Ray strolled through the door, whistling an old Backstreet Boys tune. Hawk laughed to himself before speaking.

"The things we do when we don't think anyone

is watching," Hawk said.

Ray shook his head and smiled. "I guess you finally busted me. My weakness for 90s boy bands has been exposed."

Hawk stood up. "If I was doing psychological interrogation of a suspect, I might subject them to that garbage for 24 hours straight with no sleep. And in most cases, they'd crack. But you—"

"I'd be unbreakable," Ray said. "And when you'd leave the room, I'd close my eyes and bounce to the beat."

"I don't know what happened to you, but I'm guessing your mother dropped you on the head one too many times."

"Pardon me if my music tastes aren't so wide-reaching and diverse as yours, Hawk. Will you still be my friend if I tell you I hate the Eagles?"

"Blasphemy," Hawk said. "May your life in the hereafter be filled with Macarena on endless repeat."

"I love that tune," Ray said, thrusting his arms out to begin the song's accompanying dance moves.

Hawk moaned. "I'm glad I left the Seals because I would've straight up shot you myself if you subjected me to your music at base camp."

"At least we agree that the Dallas Cowboys are the greatest football team of all time."

Hawk cocked his head to one side. "Yeah, about

the Cowboys—"

"Oh, no. Don't you dare tell me you gave up your love for America's team too. If you tell me you're a Patriots fan, I'm gonna—"

"Let's just table this discussion for now. I can see this devolving to the point where you try to tell me Stephanie Jackson wasn't the cutest girl in the seventh grade."

"It was Jennifer Preston," Ray said.

"See what I mean," Hawk said.

They both laughed and concluded the good-natured argument with a series of high fives and fist bumps.

"So, did you talk to your boss today?" Hawk asked, abruptly changing the conversation.

"I did."

"You didn't tell him my name, did you?"

"Of course not, Hawk. I know how to be discreet."

"Good because I'm going in with a new legend. I can never be too careful these days with Michaels on my tail."

"Will you have everything in place by tomorrow at noon?"

"Of course," Hawk said. "Is that when he wants to meet?"

Ray nodded. "He told me he's always open to meeting new recruits, especially ones that are trained well."

"Thanks. I really appreciate your help. All I can ask for is a chance."

"Now it's up to you to impress him. And let me tell you that Oliver Ackerman isn't easily impressed. But if anybody can do it, I'm sure you can."

* * *

HAWK AWOKE EARLY the next morning so he could check for any correspondence from Alex. He wasn't surprised to find a complete dossier workup for a former Navy Seal named Chuck Pearl with his picture attached. With an exemplary record that would impress but not overly so, Hawk's new legend seemed like a cinch to land him a job with Ackerman's security firm. Hawk printed out his prepared resume and then backtracked to eliminate his digital footprint.

The sound of the printer whirring was loud, so much so that Ray stumbled out of his bedroom and into the hall.

"What's going out here?" Ray asked as he squinted and rubbed his eyes.

"Sorry, I didn't mean to wake you," Hawk said. "I was just gathering a few things for my interview today."

Ray grunted and marched back to his room.

Hawk studied his resume, reading and re-reading it until he felt comfortable with all the details. In concocting the cover, Alex had left as many things as possible close to the truth. Hawk grinned as he perused all the points, amazed at Alex's attention to every element she included. Though their relationship wasn't of the traditional or normal variety, he appreciated how Alex not only knew her way around his files, but she also knew little nuggets about him that made his dossier feel more personal.

Alex also included an entire file about the sport of cricket for Hawk to study. She noted that Ackerman was a big fan of Kieron Pollard, one of the stars for the Mumbai Indians in the Indian Premier League. Pollard was from Trinidad, where Hawk spent a few weeks one summer as a teenager rebuilding homes ravaged by a recent hurricane.

"It'll be a great talking point," she wrote.

Hawk agreed and did his best to catch up on the T20 version of cricket, which had supplanted the traditional test version of the game.

Cricket that doesn't take five days to finish a match? No wonder the sport is suddenly becoming popular the world over.

Hawk immersed himself in the files to the point that he almost lost track of time. A gentle nudge from Ray snapped Hawk back into the present.

"You ready?" Ray asked.

"What time is it?" Hawk looked up and asked.

"It's eleven-thirty. We need to get going. If there's one thing Ackerman hates, it's tardiness."

Hawk retrieved his resume from the pile of documents he'd printed out earlier and stood up.

"Let's do it."

During the car ride to the office, Ray gave Hawk as many pointers as possible, warning him about the potential pitfalls and taboo topics.

Once they arrived, they both went through a security screening . Ray went first and seemed to have a good rapport with one of the guards, chatting about the previous day's Yankees game. Hawk followed but remained silent except when questioned.

Stay under the radar. Be forgettable.

Hawk reminded himself that this position was a means to an end, the kind of end that could lead to getting his life back if managed properly.

Ray gave Hawk a cursory tour, which consisted of a brief look at the company's warehouse, which was loaded with weapons and surveillance tech.

"Impressive," Hawk said. "You guys look like you're ready for an all-out assault from Iran."

"If it comes to that, we'll be adequately prepared," Ray said with a sly grin.

Ray led Hawk upstairs into the suite of offices, gesturing toward the couch.

"Have a seat while I let Ackerman know you're here."

Hawk complied and scanned the room. A handful of women keyed in numbers at their computer terminals, while several men scurried about the room, piling up documents on the desks. The pale walls remained bare, with the exception of a few framed motivational posters about success and excellence and victory. To Hawk, the office appeared about as sterile as possible, a corporate entity without a soul.

When Ray emerged from his boss's office, Ackerman followed suit.

Wearing a grin that Hawk deemed disingenuous, Ackerman offered his hand to Hawk. The two men shook.

"Mr. Pearl, I've heard some wonderful things about you from Ray," Ackerman said, chomping on a piece of gum. "Please, let's talk in my office."

Hawk nodded and strode toward Ackerman's office.

"Have a seat," Ackerman said as he slipped in behind Hawk and closed the door. Walking around to the back of the desk, Ackerman sat down and leaned forward, his hands clasped.

Hawk settled into his seat, sitting upright.

"Did you bring your resume with you?" Ackerman asked, holding his hand out.

Hawk gave over the documents.

"Complete with references and their contact information, I hope," Ackerman said.

"Of course. It's all right there."

Ackerman remained quiet for a moment as he perused the papers that Alex had meticulously prepared for Hawk. In relative silence, Ackerman's eyes raced across the page, stopping only to arch his eyebrows or purse his lips. Hawk had yet to discern what any of the facial movements meant, but that didn't stop him from speculating. By Hawk's count, the positive contortions outnumbered the negative ones by a count of five to two. Hawk just hoped the two negative ones didn't ultimately outweigh the positive ones.

"You've done some solid work, Chuck," Ackerman finally said as he placed the resume down on his desk. "And you seem to know your way around a weapon or two."

"I felt like that might be what would make me a strong candidate."

"Knowledge of weapons and past experience certainly bode well for you," Ackerman said. "But that's not all we do around here. For some of our more sensitive operations, I need to know that you're going to handle your more discreet assignments with great professionalism—and without a word to anyone else about what you're doing."

"I can do stealth as well as power," Hawk said. "Just call me the Keiron Pollard of the private security world."

Ackerman's eyes sparkled as he relaxed his posture.

"You follow T20 cricket as well?"

Hawk nodded. "Mostly the Indian Premier League as well as the Australian Big Bash League."

"I love the Mumbai Indians," Ackerman said.

"They've been winning a lot of titles lately, haven't they?"

Ackerman nodded. "They're building a dynasty, which has been fun to watch."

Hawk smiled, sensing that he'd been able to penetrate Ackerman's guarded self.

"Now, speaking of champions, we have quite the team here," Ackerman said. "And we've built that sense of camaraderie around our chemistry. While you have a great resume and the kind of experience we're looking for, I'm not getting a good vibe from you."

Hawk scowled. "What do you mean?"

"I mean, your credentials are sufficient, exactly what we're looking for, to be honest. But you just don't have that *it* factor I'm looking for, that little extra mojo that I see in people that they need to mesh with what we've already built here. Kind of like how Keiron Pollard is a great fit with the Indians but not with the West Indies national team. Make sense?"

Hawk shrugged. "Perhaps, though I have a great rapport with Ray. We've got a long history together and—"

"And, frankly, that's what I'm not so sure about.

I need my new hires to respect Ray. He leads guys into some difficult situations at times, and everyone on the team needs to both trust and fear him. Are you smelling what I'm stepping in?"

Hawk huffed a laugh through his nose at the southern colloquial phrase.

"I suppose, but I'm confident we can get along on the field and it won't be a problem."

Ackerman stood up. "Well, I've already made up my mind, but if that changes or another opportunity arises, I'll let you know."

He offered his hand to Hawk, who shook it and then turned toward the door.

"So, Chuck, you'll be staying with Ray for a while?" Ackerman asked.

Nodding, Hawk stopped and looked back at Ackerman.

"For a few weeks anyway. If I can't find any work here, I'll likely have to move on. Ray likes me, but probably not enough to let me mooch off him for a while."

"Well, good luck," Ackerman said. "I'll keep you in mind and maybe we'll have an opportunity for you here."

Hawk walked downstairs, where Ray was waiting.

"How'd it go?" Ray asked. "From the look on your face, I'd say not so well."

"Let's just say our prior relationship was likely what did me in; at least that's what Ackerman said."

"That's odd. He never mentioned anything about that to me before you went in for the interview."

"So this is a shock to you?" Hawk asked.

"Completely. I thought he was going to hire you."

"I'm at a loss then because I don't know what could've made him decide I wasn't capable of serving under you, if that was really the issue."

"Keep your head up," Ray said. "I have some other local contacts who might be able to take you on and pay you under the table."

"I'm not sure I want to start pumping my name out there like that. It might draw some suspicion."

"I'll be discreet. Don't worry. Oliver Ackerman is going to regret not hiring you."

Oliver Ackerman, Oliver Ackerman. For the first time since he'd reconnected with Ray, the name of his boss rang a bell.

That name suddenly sounds so familiar.

Hawk couldn't put his finger on it, but he would swear on his great grandmother's Bible that he'd heard it once before, somewhere. And from what he could recall, the name wasn't attached to a fond connotation. He needed Alex to dig into Ackerman's background and find out more about him.

Just who are you, Oliver Ackerman?

CHAPTER 4

ALEX'S EYES WIDENED with delight when she saw another message in the draft folder from Hawk. Their constant exchanges in their shared email account started to feel like old times to her, fulfilling the craving she had to get back to what she considered normal life—serving with Firestorm. Her foray into the corporate world had already started to take a toll on her soul. But for the moment, the drudgery was put aside and she focused on addressing Hawk's request.

"Dig into Oliver Ackerman?" she said under her breath. "But I already did that. I found out that he was into cricket and who his favorite team and player were."

She'd also compiled a brief overview of Ackerman's career, but apparently Hawk needed more. However, the kind of depth he was asking for could potentially set off alarm bells if she was doing it from a public computer. She needed to hack into a high-powered server to access the full extent of his records. And it wouldn't be an easy task.

Later that evening after work, she assembled a list of the best targets for such a job and whittled down the number until there were only two remaining. After much deliberation, she landed on Golden Financial, a wealth management company. She'd met several employees from there while working at Lloyd's, and hatched a plan to gain access to the building after hours.

* * *

JUST BEFORE THE CLOSE of business the next day, Alex made a delivery to one of the account executives from Golden Financial. She strode into his office and sat down for a little small talk. However, the cup of tea she brought provided her with the crucial time she needed to succeed.

"Blueberry hibiscus," Alex said as she placed the cup in front of Paul Wellman, the Golden Financial employee she knew best.

"My favorite," Wellman said, wrapping his hands around the cup. "At least, my favorite *American* tea."

"We're still trying to catch up with the British in that culinary department."

"It might be the only one that you haven't surpassed us in at this point—though if your traitors hadn't dumped crates of tea into Boston Harbor, things might be different on that front as well."

They both shared a laugh before Wellman gulped down his drink.

"What brings you over today?" he asked.

"Just the usual. I needed to discuss some security concerns we had with some of our clients."

He drank some more of his tea. "And you just decided to stop by my office and bring me tea? A bit unusual, especially for you."

"I normally don't venture out much, but this was necessary. But no need to panic. I just thought since I was here, a gesture of goodwill might be in order since you were such a gentleman to me the last time we were out together."

Wellman chuckled and then cocked his head. "Me? A gentleman? I don't think I quite recall what you're referring to?"

"You don't? The Lion's Pub downtown with some of your co-workers, who were hitting on me— you made them stop. Is any of this ringing a bell?"

Wellman shook his head. "I'm afraid I don't remember any of it."

Alex shrugged. "Maybe you were drunk too, but you were quite chivalrous in your response."

She watched him twist his wedding band before

hiding his hands beneath his desk.

"Well, maybe you can make it up to me sometime with a stiffer drink," he said, hoisting his cup in the air again before finishing it off.

"You can bring your wife along as well," Alex said.

Wellman's face went red before turning pale. He held up his finger and stood.

"If you'll excuse me, I'll be right back."

He hustled out of his office and disappeared.

Fast-acting laxatives for the win.

Alex went to work, reaching across Wellman's desk and snatching his security card. She jammed it into a device she'd hidden in her purse and started to create a cloned copy. One of the four green lights indicating the progress blinked slowly as the card reader gathered all the information.

A second light then began to blink.

Come on, come on.

She glanced into the hallway to make sure Wellman wasn't about to walk in the room. There was still no sign of him.

After about a minute, a third light joined in.

Just one more minute.

The seconds that ticked past seemed to move at glacial speeds. Alex looked once more toward the door for Wellman. He wasn't there—but Harry Sterling was.

"Alex? Alex Duncan? Is that you?" he said, leaning

against the doorjamb.

She forced a smile and nodded. "You caught me."

"What are you doing in Wellman's office? You know he's just going to refer you elsewhere," Sterling said before looking over his shoulder and then continuing in a whisper. "He's quite clueless when it comes to matters of security, despite what his title might suggest."

Alex tried to maintain eye contact and ignore the urge to glance down at her purse.

"I think he's rather knowledgeable," she said.

Sterling smiled. "He's standing right behind me, isn't he?"

She shook her head. "No, feel free to speak your mind any time—just do so at your own risk."

"Oh, God, I didn't mean it like that. It was a joke, right? Please don't say anything to Wellman. I absolutely adore him."

"Certainly doesn't sound like it."

"You Americans struggle mightily when it comes to the humor department."

Don't look down, Alex. This jerk will be gone shortly.

"We can't be great at everything, but excel when it comes to revolutions."

"You're particularly catty today," Sterling said. "Perhaps you need to loosen up after work, maybe meet me there for a pint."

"We Americans are also devoted to our work—and this American has plenty to do once I finish meeting with Wellman. So, if you'll excuse me."

Sterling chuckled. "Wellman's still not here. What did he do? Fall in when he went to the loo?"

Alex shrugged and turned back to face Wellman's desk. She noticed that the fourth light on the card reader finally lit up. It was done. All she had to do was get the card back before he returned.

Slipping her hand inside her purse, she grabbed the card and prepared to ease it onto the desk when Sterling plopped into Wellman's chair. Sterling interlocked his fingers behind his head, leaned back, and propped his feet up.

"So, tell me, Alex, what is it that you dream about at night?" Sterling asked.

"I'm not doing this with you," she said.

"Doing what? It was just a friendly question."

"Harry, you know good and well what I'm talking about. I think it's time for you to leave."

"I second that notion," Wellman said as he entered his office.

"Finally," Alex said. "Is everything all right? I was beginning to worry that you weren't coming back. I received a call that I'm needed back at the office right away and—"

"When did you receive a call?" Sterling asked. "I

never saw you answer your phone."

Wellman swatted at Sterling's legs. "Get those off my desk right now, you filthy swine."

Alex clutched the card in her hand still hidden in her purse, waiting for the precise moment to return the security card. But a good opportunity hadn't readily presented itself. With each passing second, she felt like a spotlight was being shown on her arm that was diving deep into her purse. She felt sweat beading up on her forehead.

Sterling grumbled as he complied with Wellman's wishes.

"Where is my key card?" Wellman asked as he surveyed his desk. "It was right here when I left."

Alex seized her chance.

"It's right here," she said, leaning forward in her chair as if she was picking the card up off the floor. She then hoisted Wellman's prized possession in the air.

"How on earth did it end up down there?" Wellman asked.

"Harry kicked it off when he decided to pretend to be you," Alex said.

"I did no such thing," Sterling said in an attempt to defend himself. "I was very careful with where I placed my feet on your desk."

"You weren't careful enough," Wellman said as

he gently shoved Sterling in the back. "You're such a slob. Now get out of my office before I have to call someone in a hazmat suit to remove you."

"I knocked nothing off your desk," Sterling said. "Your little American friend has quite a fanciful imagination. You won't believe what she told me about her dream last night. It was quite, how should I say it—*enlightening*?"

"I didn't tell you anything, you Cretan," Alex said. "I wouldn't be surprised if the sole reason you came by this office was to start a fight and earn a promotion simply through attrition."

"That's absurd," Sterling said.

"Just get out," Wellman said. He sighed and waited for Sterling to leave. He lingered in the doorway for a few moments.

"You're making a big mistake," Sterling said. "I'm not your villain here."

"Out—now!" Maddux said.

When Sterling finally exited the room, Wellman turned toward Alex.

"I'm sorry you had to see all that as well as endure one of Sterling's petulant tantrums."

"You don't have to apologize for his behavior," Alex said. "He can do that in his own time."

"Truly, I'm sorry about the delay. What would you like to talk about again?"

"I hate to visit and run, but I need to get going. I received a call from my office, and I need to get back for an important meeting. Let's talk again soon."

They both stood up. "Well, if there's anything I can ever help you with, please don't hesitate to call me."

"As a matter of fact, there is," Alex said.

"And what's that?" he asked.

"I need to make a stop in the ladies room before I leave."

But Alex didn't have any intention of leaving— at least not right away.

CHAPTER 5

Washington, D.C.

PRESIDENT CONRAD MICHAELS couldn't stop smiling as he watched a report on the latest poll results. Armed with data, political pundits from both sides of the aisles bickered over what the numbers meant. The ability to spin negative news into something positive was an imperative for political operatives to survive in Washington, but even the masters of their trade couldn't do much to reframe the dire news for Michaels' opponent. Michaels enjoyed watching the opposing party's minions squirm as the experts on his side gloated.

"It's not easy to polish a turd," quipped David Kriegel, Michaels' chief of staff. "That's what my father used to say whenever I brought home a bad grade and tried to explain why. He never let me finish, interrupting me with that observation."

"Your father was right," Michaels said. "When it stinks, you have to call it what it is and flush it. But those morons can't seem to do that."

"They're the ones circling in the toilet right now."

Michaels chuckled. "And come Election Day, the rest of the water will come swirling around them and bid them farewell."

Kriegel nodded. "Sounds about right—as long as we don't get an October surprise."

"An October surprise on an incumbent president? Now, that'd be quite the trick."

Kriegel arched his eyebrows and cocked his head to one side.

"You sure you don't have anything else to hide?" he asked. "I'd hate to get caught off guard by—"

"You know everything there is to know," Michaels said. "My life is an open book, both in this office and to the American people. God knows, I'm not perfect. But our country is a forgiving bunch. And if I've weathered the things I have while in office, there's nothing prior to this that's going to spell doom and gloom on my re-election campaign."

Kriegel shook his head and wagged his finger. "That's not a good approach. The minute you start to think there's no way—*boom*—that's when you get blindsided and everything goes to hell."

"I don't get blindsided. I've been in this game far

too long to let anyone sneak up on me."

"All I'm saying is don't get over confident. You've also been in politics long enough to know that the American people are a fickle bunch. One day they love you and want to name every new school, highway, and federal building after you; the next day, they want to pick over the bones of your corpse."

"Spare me the moral tales, David. I'm going to be fine."

Knocking interrupted their banter, which Michaels welcomed. Kriegel's cautious approach was helpful when he was advising Michaels' first campaign. But now Michaels needed tenacious partners who would go for the throat of his opponent—and Kriegel lacked the killer instinct.

"Why don't you get that," Michaels said, nodding toward the door.

Kriegel didn't say a word as he marched over and allowed the visitor inside.

"Thomas Miller," Michaels began, "how did you get past my secretary?"

Michaels intended his comment as a joke, but his White House aide didn't crack a smile.

"I have an urgent matter I needed to let you know about," Miller said.

"Well, enough with the dramatics," Michaels said. "Out with it."

"Sir, it's—it's kind of personal. I'm not sure you want any more people than necessary knowing."

Michaels shrugged. "I've got nothing to hide, especially with David here. If you've got something to tell me, he can hear it."

"In that case, sir, I came to tell you about a report we received through the Secret Service."

"What? An assassination threat? A terrorist plot?"

"No, sir. There is a woman claiming to be the mother of your daughter."

"That's preposterous."

Michaels cut his eyes over at Kriegel, whose eyes had widened as he stared back at the president.

"Don't look at me like that," Michaels said.

"As I was just saying . . ." Kriegel said.

"Thank you, Thomas," Michaels said. "We'll take it from here. And I appreciate your use of discretion in this instance. I don't forget that kind of loyalty."

Miller exited the room. Once the door latched shut, Kriegel stood up and started pacing.

"This is exactly the thing I was afraid of," he said.

"You're jumping to conclusions, David. This is a complete fabrication. Whoever this woman is only wants her fifteen minutes of fame and is likely being preyed upon by William Braxton's nasty operatives."

Braxton was more than just a political rival as he

squared off with Michaels twice in U.S. senate races. Michaels had never lost, but the margin wasn't a comfortable one in either election. And after Michaels won the White House, Braxton triumphed in the special election to refill the seat—and in the process, he became his party's answer to Michaels with a strong opposing voice. The fact that they were fraternity brothers in college made the rivalry personal to Michaels. Braxton took their competition to another level when he became the opposing party's nominee for president.

"You really think Braxton is behind this?" Kriegel asked.

"Your assumption is that I'm guilty, which is disappointing."

"I didn't mean to imply anything, I just—"

"Just go deal with it, okay?" Michaels said. "This doesn't have to be an October surprise, and your job is to make sure it doesn't turn into that."

"I'll do whatever I can."

Michaels walked toward the door and opened it, gesturing toward the exit as he looked at Kriegel.

"I appreciate you handling this as quietly as possible."

"Of course," Kriegel said as he exited the room.

Michaels left his office and headed straight to his assistant.

"What's the rest of my day look like?" he asked her.

She smiled. "You've got a briefing with your campaign manager in five minutes. Oh, and I also have a note for you."

She handed Michaels an envelope. He opened it as he returned to his office. Inside, he found a hand-written note scrawled across a piece of ruled paper.

Everything is in place to make the deal happen, and all we need is your green light.

Michaels folded up the message and tucked it in the inside pocket of his coat. He smiled as he eased into the chair behind his desk.

Have I got an October surprise for you, Will Braxton.

CHAPTER 6

Brighton, England

ALEX RUBBED HER CALVES as they started to burn. She'd been perched on the toilet in a locked stall for nearly three hours. After she was convinced the office would be virtually empty, she eased onto the floor and dug into her purse for her wig, sunglasses, and gloves. She donned the disguise and ventured back into the hallway. Her assumption proved true as the floor was empty.

She approached the server room, using Wellman's duplicated access card to gain entrance. As Goldman Financial's cyber security chief, Wellman was in charge of making sure none of the company's information was compromised through hacks. But she doubted he would ever anticipate an onsite hacking job, especially by someone he was fond of.

Wasting no time, Alex went to work. She hammered away on the keyboard in search of the truth about Michaels and Oliver Ackerman. Masking her location through a series of redirects, she eventually used a backdoor portal to hack into the NSA's database. She broke through several firewalls and uncovered a treasure trove of information regarding Ackerman. She used a small digital camera to take picture after picture of documents about the private security head from Oman.

While Alex felt comfortable navigating around on the NSA's server, she didn't want to press her luck and overstay her welcome. Her best guess was that she had no more than two minutes to shut down her session and get out of there before someone at the NSA figured out where she was as well as what she was doing. In an effort to further cover her tracks, she searched for unrelated issues, some of which appeared to dig deep into Michaels. At a cursory glance, she wanted anyone looking at her breadcrumbs to be convinced that she was digging for dirt on Michaels and that Ackerman just happened to be an entry point into the search.

She glanced at her watch—less than a minute.

Alex typed furiously, rooting around in one final folder. Her mouth fell agape as she read the details of the documents in front of her. Her hunch had been right.

She took a few final pictures before terminating

her access. Before logging out, she deleted all of the security footage from earlier in the day that could've linked her with any piece of clothing she wore.

Placing her camera back in her purse, she slung it over her shoulder and slipped into the hallway. As she moved down the corridor, the only thing she heard was the low hum of the fluorescent bulbs. But as she neared the elevator, she heard something else— a squeaky wheel.

Alex rushed over to the wall and stood flush against it. She peeked around the corner to assess the situation. About twenty meters away, an elderly man with his head down wheeled a yellow bucket down the hall using the mop's handle to steer. Though unaware of Alex's presence, he guided his pail in her direction.

Think, Alex. Think.

She'd managed to glide through Goldman Financial after hours as if she was a virtual ghost, but she was about to be exposed by the one thing she hadn't considered—a janitor. She spun on her heels and eased back down the hall, trying door after door. They were all locked.

Come on, come on.

With each handle she jiggled, the results remained the same. The doors didn't budge. Alex felt her pulse quicken with each squeak emitted by the old man's bucket. The sound echoed off the empty walls.

Alex concluded that she would have to wait out the old man and pray that the security guard wasn't watching the cameras closely enough. Her movements would create suspicion, but she felt powerless to change that. She walked backward until she came to another intersection and hid around the corner.

The noisy wheels then fell eerily silent.

Alex leaned against the wall, resisting the urge to sneak a peek.

What's going on?

She couldn't look, at least not yet. There were a number of reasons why the custodian had put on the brakes. Perhaps he'd run into a security guard or another employee, though she hadn't seen either. Maybe he was resting. At the rate he moved, she was surprised that he was still employed, much less that he could accomplish his assignment efficiently, if at all. Alex felt a conflicting mix of pity for the man as well as anger that he was meddling in her plan, albeit unbeknownst.

The silence was replaced with the jangling of keys, followed by the creak of a door opening. Alex mustered up the courage to look around the corner and watched as he drove his bucket in a nearby room. The door shut with an echoing thud.

Alex darted down the hall and entered the stairwell located next to the elevators. She descended the steps, exiting the building in the second level of the parking garage. She eased along the wall, well out of the view of the sole security guard roaming the premises. She slipped out onto the sidewalk and checked her surroundings to see if anyone had spotted her.

"Finally," she muttered under her breath. "In the clear."

She sauntered down the street as if she was coming back from a night of shopping, though a fruitless one based on the lack of bags draped off her arms. With hunger pangs gnawing at her, she decided to go to her favorite restaurant.

Confident that danger had subsided, she hadn't checked over her shoulder for a few blocks on the sparsely populated Brighton streets. But it didn't matter, as the person who grabbed her surprised her by coming out of one of the alleyways.

The attacker clamped a gloved hand over her mouth and dragged her off the street.

Alex wanted to scream but something made her reconsider, something about the man's smell. He turned her around and Alex was face to face with J.D. Blunt.

"You were careless tonight," Blunt said.

"How did you—" she stammered.

"Never mind that, but we shouldn't be seen walking together on the street. It's too risky. Meet me around the corner at the café, Winston's Place, in fifteen minutes. I'll be at the table in the back corner."

Alex nodded and gave him a hug.

"Don't ever scare me like that again," she said. "You don't know what I could've done to you."

"I'm sure I would've been able to handle it."

"Even with that limp of yours?" she asked, gesturing toward his leg.

"My limp isn't a handicap, but it is a great way to make sure everyone underestimates me."

"So your limp is faked?"

Blunt smiled. "See you in fifteen minutes."

He hobbled out of the alley and started in a direction that was a circuitous route.

* * *

WHEN ALEX SAT DOWN in the booth across from Blunt, she expected him to be excited about the information she'd uncovered on Ackerman and Michaels. She explained how Hawk believed that Ackerman's security firm was involved with the DOD in some way. But he barely flinched when she told him.

"I didn't know they were connected, but I would've guessed it," Blunt said. "If there's a sketchy American in the Middle East who has ties to someone in Washington, my money would always be on Michaels."

"You don't look surprised," she said.

"Not at all. I've been around far too long to get genuinely shocked by anything. Speaking of things I'm not shocked by, I've got something else I want to talk with you about."

"Have you heard from my brother?"

Blunt shook his head. "Sadly, I haven't heard anything on Samuels yet. I'm not sure what's going on with him. I've placed calls to several of my more reliable sources, but so far I've come up with a big fat goose egg."

"So what is it you want to tell me?"

"It's the real reason I wanted to meet with you."

"The kind of reason you think was worth taking this kind of chance?"

Blunt nodded. "I know the owner here, but even if I didn't, I would've tried to meet with you."

"Now you've got me worried."

"You should be, though we also all have a reason for hope as a result."

"This ought to be interesting."

Blunt smiled. "I got a tip from one of my insiders about what Michaels is planning on doing next—arming Al Hasib."

Alex's mouth fell agape. "You've gotta be kidding."

"I wish I was, but that bastard thinks selling arms to Al Hasib is the way to keep this conflict fresh in the minds of the American people. The more firepower Al Hasib has, the more damage they'll be able to inflict on us."

"And how does this help Michaels?"

"He gets to ride in on the white horse and save the day, just in time for the election."

Alex crinkled her nose and narrowed her eyes. "That man makes me sick."

"Well, he's going to make us all dead if we let him continue this reckless display of leadership."

"Don't demean the word *leadership* by associating it with Michaels' actions."

Blunt chuckled. "You seem so indifferent about this whole subject, Alex."

"If he were here right now, I'm not sure anyone could stop me from taking Michaels out."

"You're starting to sound like an assassin. Let's leave all the dirty work for Hawk since he's so efficient at it."

Alex sighed. "This is not right. It's a heinous crime against the American people. Someone should out him for that right now. Our country deserves to know the truth about the man sitting in the Oval Office."

"They will—but in due time. We don't want to alert everyone about this just yet."

Alex could feel her face getting warmer and was undoubtedly turning red with rage.

"And why not?" she asked.

"This is also our way out, the way we're going to get our lives back."

"You're gonna have to explain that one to me because from where I'm sitting it seems like Michaels is just gonna get what he wants without any fallout or consequences. I swear if that sonofabitch was sitting where you are right now, I'd—"

"Why don't we put him in that chair then?" Blunt said.

"Is he tied up outside in a van? Because if that's the case, I say let's do it."

"No, he's still hidden in the Middle East. But if you put your computer skills to good work, we'll have a decent shot at stopping him."

"And how do you know that?"

"I know when and where they're going to meet—and now thanks to you and Hawk, I know who they are planning on meeting with."

"Suppose we're able to stop this sale. What exactly do you hope is going to come out of such an operation, aside from the natural consequences?"

Blunt shrugged. "Ultimately, I hope I regain my freedom, though nothing is a given at this point. Knowing Michaels, he's liable to turn us into heroes. But at least we'll have the truth."

"Possessing the truth isn't the same as acting on it day after day."

"Let me ask you a question, Alex. Suppose you have the opportunity to get your life back in exchange for a small lie. Would you do it?"

"Depends on how small and what the lie is about."

"Good," Blunt said, slapping the table. "Your moral relativism might just be what we need to snare the man and expose Michaels—two birds with one stone."

Alex flashed a sly grin. "And you're sure we can do that?"

"I'm sure of nothing except that I'm on the side of truth and justice. But if we can expose this right before the election, it just might be enough to make him lose."

"And you think that will keep him from coming after us?"

"It will if he's behind bars."

Alex rolled her eyes. "A U.S. president in prison? That'll be the day. Besides, he's not going to lose the election. He's the Teflon man, remember? No scandal ever seems to stick to him."

"You be ready because we're not only going to make this one stick, we're going to make it swallow him whole. Michaels will forever be remembered as the most traitorous president in American history."

"I'm not sure if I share your faith, but I'll be ready. Anything to get out of this life of pushing numbers and back to doing what we all do best."

Blunt nodded. "All I need you to do is get him on record talking about this weapons sale. It's that simple."

"I've got the perfect technology for that."

"Make it happen, Alex. And don't miss. We're only going to get one shot at this."

Blunt threw some cash on the table and got up, leaning heavily on his stick.

"Do you really need that thing?" she asked, gesturing toward Blunt's cane.

"Define the word *need*," he said with a wink before he hobbled toward the door.

The brief moment of levity was a welcome respite for Alex after her heavy conversation with Blunt. The task ahead of her was grave, as would be the consequences if everything didn't go off without a hitch.

CHAPTER 7

Muscat, Oman

HAWK OPENED THE JOINT email account and read over the note Alex had posted in the draft folder. The instructions posted seemed odd given that she warned him that they shouldn't speak on the phone. But she swore it was an emergency and time was of the essence. Most of all, she promised no one would be able to listen in on their conversation since she would be utilizing a protocol that would be impossible to trace or listen to without a filter. Though Hawk felt uneasy about Alex's last request—use a program to mask your voice.

Despite his misgivings, Hawk decided to go along with the plan. After all, he'd just be following her directions, which he assumed had to be issued by Blunt since she would never act alone. Plus, he had a way to make sure that she was really Alex and not someone who'd just gained access to the joint account somehow.

At the prescribed time, Hawk logged onto Ray's computer and precisely followed Alex's detailed action points.

"Hello," Alex said, sounding like a cross between a bullfrog and a chipmunk.

Hawk started chuckling.

"Don't laugh," she said. "It's all for your own good."

"Just don't tell me that you're my father," Hawk deadpanned.

"So, you really think I sound like Darth Vader?"

"Maybe Darth Vader's wife."

"You think I sound like Natalie Portman talking through a ventilator?"

Hawk grinned. "Before I answer that question, you need to answer something for me."

"Okay. Go ahead."

Hawk needed to make sure that Alex was truly on the other end—and he knew one way to ensure that she was.

"In the movie *Laagan*, who starred as Bhuvan and also served as the film's producer?"

"You really think that's going to stump me?" she asked.

"I'm not trying to stump you—just anyone else

who's pretending to be you."

"In that case, it's Aamir Khan. And that's a great movie, by the way," she said. "After I watched it, I actually wanted to play cricket."

"Okay, continue," Hawk said. "I know it's you, by both your answer and the fact that you were inspired to play that sport after watching the movie."

"You know me well, don't you?"

"I do," Hawk said as he chuckled. "Now, get on with it. What's so important?"

"Those schematics that you saw are likely tied to a weapons deal that's going down soon."

"And who's behind all of this?"

"I'll give you three guesses and the first two don't count."

"Michaels. That bastard is always meddling in things he has no business messing with."

"In his quest to win votes and make the world a safer place, he's ironically about to make it far more dangerous."

"And hopefully lose enough votes to lose the upcoming general election."

"That's what I'm hoping, at least."

Hawk nodded resolutely. "So, what do you need me to do?"

"Nothing big. I just need you to record your friend's boss for a total of one minute."

"That's it?"

"It needs to be in person, of course."

Hawk moaned. "I knew there'd be a catch somewhere."

"Is that gonna be a problem?"

"Of course not. I'll figure something out."

"Good," she said. "Just upload the files to the usual place."

"I'll try to have something to you within 48 hours."

"Hurry because we don't have much time."

Hawk terminated the program he was using to communicate with Alex and hid his steps on the computer. He migrated over to the living room and fell back onto the couch. He needed a plan to get Ackerman to talk, though Hawk doubted he could get the time of day out of Michaels' puppet from the Middle East.

"How do I get Ackerman's attention?" Hawk asked himself aloud.

An idea came out of nowhere and he smiled.

"This just might work."

* * *

AS SOON AS RAY returned home from work, Hawk darted out the door, claiming to need to run a few errands. Part of his statement was true. Hawk needed to grab a few items at the grocery store—as well as record Ackerman's voice so Alex could work her magic with the recording. She'd been short on details, and Hawk didn't feel like talking over such an open line. No matter how secure Alex swore it was, it seemed like an ill-advised action.

The outside of Fortress Security appeared to be a fortified location, though it was far from being impenetrable, despite what the website claimed. Hawk surveyed the situation and considered his next move.

On top of the compound wall were two men, both armed with machine guns and decked out with enough ammo to eliminate several strongholds in any line of defense.

Maybe I should've consulted with Alex first about this.

Hawk still had time to back away and regroup. But based on what he observed during his first trip to the firm's headquarters, he was confident he could navigate his way through the perimeter.

Instead of using bullets, Hawk had gathered a pocketful of tranquilizer darts he'd found lying around Ray's house. Quieter and far less messy than the aftermath of gunshots, Hawk also saw the use of tranqs as a way to endear himself to Ackerman. Asking for a job was one thing, but doing it after you killed half his crew was another—and would likely end in either some sort of legal action or arrest.

From the position Hawk took up at the base of

the wall, he recognized how little time he had to eliminate the targets. Two guards circled the wall, while another sat perched high above the compound in a guard tower. In the half hour Hawk noted their routes, they seemed to pass by each other every four minutes. Putting a dart in their back was imperative to evade capture. While the guard in the tower was far less watchful, the sound of two captains dropping along the wall would surely get his attention. Hawk figured he'd have less than thirty seconds to shoot him as well.

Here goes nothing.

Hawk strode toward the wall and waited until the two men passed by each other. In one smooth motion, he unholstered his gun and fell the two guards in three shots. The guard in the tower poked his head out and started yelling frantically. Before he could return inside and call for help, Hawk had drilled the man in the neck, dropping him almost instantly.

Hawk proceeded to scale the wall and snagged two more guns of the men he'd taken down. He crept across the commons area, his gun drawn and eyes scanning his surroundings. When he heard the trampling of feet coming from his right, he darted toward an armored vehicle parked to his left. The guards fanned out along the edge of the perimeter, guns trained in front of them. In their effort to capture the intruder, they left only one man to guard the office entrance.

The overconfidence of a supposed fortress never ceases to amaze me.

Hawk grabbed a rock off the ground and hurled it to the guard's left. He immediately turned in that direction, which was all the time Hawk needed to rush toward the door. By the time the guard heard Hawk coming, it was too late. Hawk had already fired a dart at the man and hit him at the base of his neck. He moaned softly while crumpling to the ground, but the muted cry for help wasn't loud enough to get his colleague's attention.

Hawk's appearance in the office lobby startled the man behind the reception desk. Clumsily, he reached for his gun.

"I wouldn't do that if I were you," Hawk said. "Now, show me where Mr. Ackerman's offices are."

The man stood and held his hands up in a posture of surrender.

"Follow me," he muttered.

The man led Hawk up a flight of stairs and pointed toward the end of the hallway.

"Now, we're going in together," Hawk said.

Hawk urged the man forward, jamming a gun into his back.

"You better knock," the man said.

Hawk ignored him and opened the door. Using the man as a shield, Hawk pressed forward and quickly understood why the man had suggested knocking.

Armed with a semi-automatic weapon, Ackerman sat behind his desk, gun trained on the entrance.

"Sorry to barge in on you like this," Hawk began, "but I don't intend you any harm."

"Tell that to the men I watched you drop from my office window."

"Tranquilizers," Hawk said, holding his gun up in the air. He knelt down and put it on the floor, kicking it over to Ackerman. Discreetly, Hawk began recording their conversation.

"What is the meaning of this?" Ackerman asked.

"I just wanna talk."

"There are better ways to set up a meeting among professionals."

"Not in our line of work," Hawk said. "You can read the resume of Chuck Pearl a hundred times, but until you see me in action, you have no clue if I'm legit or not."

Ackerman waved with the back of his hand, dismissing the man who'd led Hawk upstairs. The man scurried out of the room. Ackerman set his gun down on his desk.

"I'm not gonna lie—that was impressive," Ackerman said. "Ray told me you had some mad skills, but who wouldn't say that about his friend?"

"I understand your reticence, sir," Hawk said.

"But I'm desperate and thought I'd try another approach."

"It's also a stunt that could've led to somebody ending up dead inside my compound and creating the kind of problem I don't need from the local government."

"I admit that my actions were risky to some degree, but I never felt there was any danger of anyone getting killed. I was in control the entire time."

"What if I had some other protocols that you weren't aware of? Then what?"

"I did my homework, sir—like I always do whenever I'm assigned to a job."

Hawk hated lying in such an egregious manner, but he didn't want to admit that he winged it and had easily penetrated Ackerman's precious fortress with some on-the-go reconnaissance. In Hawk's assessment, the outfit was well armed but poorly trained. The guards could stand days of more instruction, but he figured stating the obvious might not be the smartest move. Playing to Ackerman's ego suited Hawk's purposes more.

"Not a single shot fired by one of my men," Ackerman said.

"Was that by design?"

Ackerman shook his head. "I told them to kill you on site, which must mean they never saw you or had a clear shot. Like I said, impressive."

"So, do you have an opening for me now?"

Ackerman chuckled. "Chuck, you are a tenacious one, aren't you? But unfortunately, I don't. However, I know how to reach you if something comes up. And I have a feeling something might be opening up very soon."

"I appreciate any consideration you might give me," Hawk said, nodding in a reverent fashion.

"You got it, Chuck. I'll talk to you soon. Just next time you want to follow up on an interview, I'd advise you pick up the phone first."

Hawk grinned. "And would you have picked up yours if I'd called?"

Ackerman winked and pointed at Hawk. "You've got a point. Now get out of here."

Hawk knelt down and picked his gun up off the floor before tucking it in the back of his pants.

"One more thing before you go, Chuck," Ackerman said.

Hawk turned around. "What's that?"

"Try not to hurt any more of my men on your way out."

"Not a problem, sir."

After exiting Ackerman's office, Hawk hustled down the steps. He gave the man at the receptionist desk an informal salute and continued outside. As Hawk walked by the guards milling around the commons area, several of them glared at him. He smiled and issued another salute before a guard posted at the entrance begrudgingly opened the gate.

Hawk glanced over his shoulder as the chain link access fence slammed shut again. An armed guard gave Hawk a special salute, one of the middle finger variety before spitting in his direction.

Touchy bunch of wussies. Not sure if I want to work with them.

Serving under Ackerman wasn't the point of Hawk's exercise. He simply wanted to record the Fortress Security boss's voice for a full minute. And in that case, Hawk's mission was a rousing success. Hawk had captured closer to three minutes of Ackerman talking about plenty of things and doing it with a grave tone to witty banter.

Alex is gonna love me for this.

Hawk marched back toward the nearest bus stop, though he wasn't sure that was the smartest move given that he was carrying a loaded gun. The fact that it only shot tranquilizers wouldn't make any difference to the men who held every westerner suspect. If he kept his head down, he'd likely be fine. But he decided against taking a chance. He felt safer walking down sketchy streets with his gun readily available rather than being cooped up on a bus where the appearance of a gun would likely mean he would be shot or attacked by someone not so forgiving.

Dusk fell hard in Muscat. The dimly lit streets represented a far more treacherous walk home than Hawk had first imagined when he struck off for the Fortress Security offices. Men gathered in the doorsteps of closed business and smoked while discussing the day's events. Hawk understood enough Arabic to catch short snippets of their conversation topics as well as when they stopped and mentioned something related to "the American."

Most of the men appeared harmless and wouldn't stand a chance against Hawk. But it wasn't even one of the more threatening men who caught Hawk's eye. The shifty young man in his early 20s arrested Hawk's attention. He watched as the kid's eyes cut back and forth between Hawk and someone trailing a few feet behind.

Hawk maintained his composure and walked on, scanning each new street with every turn. He sought the best location to duck into before ambushing whoever was following him. Up ahead on Hawk's right, he noticed an ideal location. A dumpster jutted out of an alleyway, providing the right amount of cover for an attack.

Hawk increased his pace, trying to size up the uninvited guest by glancing in the glass storefronts. However, they were mostly covered with graffiti, making it nearly impossible to gain any kind of idea about possible suspects. A slight interruption in the letters plastered on the glass gave Hawk just enough space to catch a glimpse.

Picking up speed again, Hawk put just enough room between him and his aggressive stalker. In a flash, Hawk slid to the right of the dumpster and quickly eased his way up against the wall, hiding himself in the alleyway from any person.

Hawk listened as the footsteps that clicked past stopped when they reached the end of the dumpster and turned in his direction.

This ought to be fun.

Hawk pressed his face against the ground, viewing the man's gait to ascertain his pace. Once Hawk registered the man's plodding speed, he timed a dive into the man's legs, knocking him off balance. The two men traded several punches before Hawk delivered a flurry of them to gain the upper hand. But the vicious blow to the attacker's throat sent him reeling.

Hawk reached for his gun before he noticed it lying on the floor. When he knelt down to pick it up, the man kicked Hawk in the face. Surprised by the blow, Hawk shook his head in an attempt to regain his bearings. Before he looked up, he heard a mechanical click, the kind he'd heard many times right before a knife fight ensured. He rolled to his left as he felt the man's presence overhead. Hawk swept the man's legs out from under him, toppling him to the ground.

Hawk bounced up and scanned the ground for his gun, which he couldn't locate. Searching the area, he glanced over at the attacker groaning as he staggered to his feet. Then Hawk finally noticed the gun—in the man's hand.

"Oliver Ackerman says hello," the man said before he fired a tranquilizer dart at Hawk, who dove to the ground.

The man seemed surprised that a bullet didn't explode out of the gun's barrel, almost as surprised as Hawk was that the attacker had missed from such a short range.

Hawk took advantage of the man's stunned reaction and kicked the gun free. Without wasting another second, Hawk followed the kick with a combination of punches to the man's face. As the man reeled backward, he pulled out his knife again and swiped at Hawk. But the jabs never connected with Hawk, who evaded them before crippling the man with a brutal kick to his knee. The man hit the ground in pain, moaning and clutching his leg.

Hawk snatched the knife off the ground and stabbed the man in his leg before shooting him with the final tranquilizer dart in the neck. After a few seconds, the man passed out.

Hawk grabbed the man's cell phone and took a picture before sending it to Ackerman with a brief message. "Was this supposed to be a test?" Hawk typed and sent along with the photo. He stuffed the phone into the man's pocket and hustled down the street.

CHAPTER 8

United Nations
New York, NY

PRESIDENT MICHAELS STRODE to the podium and held up his hand in an effort to stop the applause from the United Nations General Assembly ambassadors. His humble gesture belied the way he basked in the adulation. Neither the previous U.S. president nor the one before him had ever received such a warm welcome. Michaels considered the support a direct result of his strong leadership among the international community, dismissing the political pundits who explained his popularity by the way he kowtowed to the prevailing winds blowing in Europe.

Michaels smiled and waved as he waited patiently for the clapping to cease. He surveyed the global crowd and felt his confidence swell. The U.N. had invited him to speak on the innovations he had directed in the area of renewable energy sources. But Michaels never intended to stay fully on topic.

"Mr. Secretary General, Mr. President, world leaders, and distinguished delegates—I am honored to stand up here today and address what I feel like is the defining issue of our time. Clean and renewable energy sources have the ability to transform our planet, revitalizing cities that have been ravaged by pollution as well as energizing countries that have never had the same opportunity to launch forward economically into the twenty-first century. And while I think it's important to discuss these issues, I find these technological advances even more vital to doing something we've all dreamed of. In fact, the real reason you're all here today was because of a dream long ago by some men with excellent foresight. They wanted to see the days of world wars end as well as regional conflicts. They wanted us all to dwell in peace and harmony, making the world a better place instead of one more divided by everything from ethnicity to economics to environs.

"When the world ethos is governed by men and women who care more about the future of the human race than they do lining their pockets, we have an incredible opportunity to move forward as a species, reaching and surpassing the dreams of those innovators who came before us. However, truly advancing globally requires bold leadership to create a clean environmental revolution. And none of that will be possible if we don't simultaneously root out the evil forces of terrorism."

A buzz began to fill the auditorium as Michaels' tone turned decisively off topic.

"Quite frankly, we need all of you to combat terrorism more than we need you to invent more green technologies. There are plenty of brilliant minds who conjure up ideas each day to make our world a cleaner place to live in. But there are also corrupt minds who constantly plot and scheme how to enforce their extreme beliefs on others, utilizing the tool of terrorism to do so. And that must be stopped.

"I'm proud of the advances we've made in the area of addressing terrorists all across the globe who seek to impose their brand of horror on the American people as well as our trusted allies. We will not take a passive stance on this during my tenure in the White House. Al Hasib and other groups who hope to impose fear on the global community will receive their comeuppance. No longer will we address such provocative rhetoric with attempts to merely thwart their forthcoming attacks. Today, I put forth a new resolve led by my administration and this country. Terrorists, you have nowhere to hide. We will find you and destroy you. Our actions will be swift and decisive, and you will know where we stand on your tactics designed to kill innocent people while dealing in the currency of fear. No, you will fear us. This country and any other allies who wish to join us will be protected by a union of resolve that will take aim at your pathetic attempts to sow discord and terror among the masses. We will wipe you off the face of the earth."

Michaels nodded toward one of the Secret Service agents standing off stage to his left. He hustled onto stage and walked off with Michaels.

However, the applause was somewhat muted, which confused Michaels. He'd never considered that his topic might create a backlash at worst or even just a lukewarm reception at best. He fully expected to hear a triumphant standing ovation.

"Why aren't they standing?" he asked the agent.

"Perhaps the translation is still being processed. Sometimes it can take up to thirty seconds before the words are translated."

Michaels nodded. "That must be what it is."

They disappeared offstage where Michaels met David Kriegel.

"So, how did I do?" Michaels asked with a wide grin.

"Why the hell did you go off script? You were supposed to talk about green technologies—that was it."

"Never let a rapt audience go to waste," Michaels said. "I couldn't care less what those bureaucratic bozos out there think of me. That was for the American people. That was for my campaign."

"You're already ahead in the polls. Why do something that's not going to engender goodwill across the board?"

"Vying for voters across the board doesn't get you elected," Michaels said. "But pandering to the majority opinion is one way to divide and conquer."

"But everyone thinks we should fight terrorism," Kriegel said. "Even your opponent is a staunch believer in that."

"He can't demonstrate action, but I can."

"Heaven forbid you have something planned."

Michaels smiled. "Heaven won't be able to stop the hell I have planned for a certain group of terrorists in the Middle East. It's going to make for terrific television."

"I don't even want to ask."

"Good, then don't. I just know that voters will definitely pull the lever for me on Election Day if they feel like they're going to be safer with me as their commander in chief."

"This is absurd. I didn't agree to stay on another term so you could retain the White House with bullshit fear-mongering tactics."

"The only thing that matters about political tactics are if they work or not. Besides, no one ever claimed that politics was a sanitized profession."

Kriegel sighed as he hung his head. "We might be through here."

"You gonna quit on me now?" Michaels said. "You've done a fantastic job, David. All I did out there today was seal the deal—Well, it'll be sealed in a few days after I back up my talk with action."

"And how exactly are you going to do that?"

Michaels wagged his finger. "No, no, no. You said you weren't going to ask."

"You're right. I did. Forget I ever said anything."

"So you're still on board, right? I am going to be president again—and you'll be justly rewarded for your allegiance. At the end of the day, I'm a far better ally than I am an enemy."

One of Michaels' aides approached the two men and held out a cell phone.

"It's for you, sir," the man said as he handed the phone to Michaels. "The caller said it's urgent."

"Yes," Michaels said.

"That was a nice speech, sir."

"Ollie, so nice of you to give me a call."

"I watched your speech online. It was a thing of beauty, sir."

"So, what do you need? I'm presuming you didn't

just call me to heap praises on my speech-making ability."

"No, I wanted to talk about the delivery you want me to make."

"What about it?"

"I'm getting nervous, sir."

"About what?"

"That this might be a setup of some sort."

Michaels chuckled. "A setup? By who?"

"I don't want to deliver the weapons—uh, package, if we're going to be placed in a compromising position."

"Did you read the message I sent you from my secure phone?"

"Yes, sir. I just—"

"Stop wasting my time. Make the tough call. That's what leaders do."

"I understand, sir. However, I wanted to let you know that everything is ready to go. All I need is the green light for the mission."

"I feel like we've already had this conversation. I told you that I'll send you the orders to move forward when it's time. Are we clear?"

"Crystal, sir."

"Good. Now stay safe out there."

Michaels hung up and walked across the room before handing the phone back to his aide.

"Everything all right?" Kriegel asked as he approached Michaels.

"Just a few more days, David, and everything will be more than all right. Just a few more days."

CHAPTER 9

Brighton, England

ALEX RUBBED HER HANDS together, her eyes wide with excitement. She couldn't remove the grin from her face if she wanted to. Utilizing her powerful software, she managed to transform her voice into Oliver Ackerman's—and President Michaels remained oblivious throughout the entire conversation. For a moment, she started to wonder if he had caught on to her ruse. But then she considered that Michaels' arrogance would likely never allow him to admit he'd been duped.

Pride cometh before a fall.

She smiled as she tightened up the audio file and made copies. After dropping several versions of the recording in various folders located in clouds around the Internet, she saved one onto a thumb drive and contemplated her next move. Ever since she hatched the plot, she was convinced it would work. But to be sitting at her computer with the power she'd been trying to attain in her hands—the moment felt somewhat surreal to her.

Part of her wanted to blast the story to all of the media from an anonymous account and be done with it. She considered sending it to Wikileaks and letting the media fight over the crumbs of the story. Despite her desire to move on to other issues that demanded her attention, this story needed to be walked into a news outlet and told by a journalist respected by everyone.

However, there was one portion of the recorded phone call that bothered her, the part about Michaels claiming to have already sent a message.

What did Michaels say?

That was the question she wanted answered at the moment, though she believed there was enough incriminating evidence to bring about public ire. Once a journalist linked "Ollie" to Oliver Ackerman, the questions would mount faster than an avalanche storming down a mountainside and envelop Michaels just the same. The final hurdle Alex faced was selecting the perfect journalist.

She couldn't pick a partisan hack or even a serious writer from an oft-dismissed news outlet. This story needed a respected political writer, one with a penchant for breaking stories and free from the trappings of political bias.

I know just the person.

Alex took a deep breath and dialed Brian Lawton's number from *The Chicago Tribune*.

She'd met Lawton in college at Northwestern University, and while they hadn't been close friends, she was still comfortable with calling him up out of the blue. After she spent a few minutes explaining the bombshell story and evidence she possessed, he stopped her.

"Should we really be talking about this on the phone?" Lawton asked. "With the precedent already set by the government for listening in on journalists' calls, I'm not really comfortable with continuing this conversation, much less even writing such a story. Now, if you want to call me some other time to reminisce about the good ole days, you can. But if you'll excuse me, I've got work to do."

Alex listened as the line went dead. She hung up, disappointed that she'd made such a mistake. If Michaels had *The Chicago Tribune's* lines monitored, the brief explanation she gave would raise red flags. Lawton was smart to get off the line.

But as Alex considered his parting words, she realized he was sending her a message. The Good Ole Days was a bar they used to frequent near campus—

and one apparently Lawton still visited on occasion. She still had the number memorized from calling to see if certain friends had beat her to their favorite gathering place.

She waited a couple of hours before calling Good Ole Days. Lonnie Cooper, the same man who'd owned the bar when she attended Northwestern, answered the phone.

"Hi, Lonnie. I'm looking for Brian Lawton," Alex said. "Is he there by chance?"

"Who is this?"

"It's your favorite Wildcat."

"Well, I'll just leave that right there and won't make any guesses."

"Lonnie, you tell all the girls that, don't you?"

Lonnie chuckled. "It's how I keep all my customers. They all think they're my favorite here. Now, who were you looking for again?"

"Brian Lawton."

"He just sat down at the bar. Hold on a second."

Alex listened as the familiar background sounds filtered through the receiver. She could hear the pings of the pinball machine in the background, two men arguing loudly in what sounded like a sports debate, and a patron trying to get Lonnie's attention for another round.

"You got my message," Lawton said as he answered the phone.

"Sorry about that. A momentary lapse in judgment. I just wasn't thinking."

"I heard you were a spy now of some sort."

"Not at the moment," Alex said. "What I'm doing now might be considered treasonous by some. But when the truth comes out, everyone will know what kind of patriot I am."

"You're likely just a decent human being above all else," Lawton said.

"I don't care what you call me as long as you don't include my name in the article. This is going to blow the lid off Michaels' campaign."

"You send me whatever you got, and I'll get everything verified before I even take this to my editor," he said.

"Good because the last journalist we tried to convince to take a story of this magnitude didn't fare so well."

"What happened to him?"

Alex sighed. "I probably shouldn't tell you this since it might make you reconsider."

"What? Did he wind up dead?"

Alex remained silent.

"Seriously, Alex. He died?"

"Yeah. The official report was suicide, but that wasn't an outright lie."

"I don't care," Lawton said. "I'll do it anyway.

Partisan politics aside, I've always had an uneasy feeling about him, like he'd somehow gamed his way into the White House."

"Well, he's trying to game his way into a second term—and he doesn't even need to based on the latest polls."

"Let's make sure that doesn't happen then."

"Good. I'll be in touch tomorrow with details on where you can pick up the assets for the story."

Alex hung up and pumped her first.

Michaels was going to go down in a glorious blaze.

CHAPTER 10

Muscat, Oman

JUST OVER TWENTY-FOUR hours after penetrating Fortress Security's headquarters, Hawk crouched against the edge of the building across the street from Ray's apartment. Deciding his next move wasn't easy given the circumstances. As a person, Hawk liked Ray. They'd definitely had their differences while in Navy Seal training, but Hawk had grown to respect his fellow soldier. Yet Hawk couldn't dismiss the nagging feeling that Ray's loyalty to Ackerman exceeded any goodwill accumulated while serving together. In short, Hawk spent the night on the street because of his distrust for Ray.

Yet Hawk's fondness for Ray as a person created a personal dilemma, one that Hawk struggled with before choosing self-preservation over a fragile friendship.

After a few minutes, Ray exited his apartment and headed down the street. With his hands stuffed in his jacket, he cast frequent glances over his shoulder until he disappeared from sight.

Hawk waited another minute and checked the street, which was empty and lit only by the pale fluorescent street lamps. He stood up and hustled toward Ray's apartment and used the key he'd been given to unlock the door. In an effort to remain discreet, Hawk kept the lights off. He rummaged through the bedroom dresser in search of some cash.

Ray has to have some emergency money stashed around here somewhere.

Frustrated at coming up empty, Hawk headed toward another room before he heard an awkward squeak beneath one of the floor planks. Hawk knelt down and used a knife to jimmy open the loose board. About a foot below was a small treasure trove—cash, weapons, and passports.

Maybe Ray doesn't trust Ackerman as much as I thought.

Hawk scooped out a healthy portion of cash before replacing the plank and securing it. With his mission accomplished, Hawk exited the apartment and walked down the empty street toward a location several blocks away that he'd seen advertising an apartment for rent. He knocked on the door several times before it swung open. An elderly man looked Hawk up and down before asking him what he wanted. After waving a wad of cash in front of the man's face, Hawk signed the papers for a monthly rental on an apartment.

* * *

HAWK DECIDED TO LAY LOW for a couple of days after he'd infiltrated Fortress Security. Severely injuring one of the thugs Ackerman had sent after Hawk wouldn't exactly endear himself to the company's boss. But Hawk had come to the conclusion that his work was done. He'd yet to contact Alex and find out how her operation went, but he decided the best move for the time being was to regroup and form a plan to get out of the Middle East. Oman had provided cover at a time when he needed it most, but he was growing weary of being watched everywhere he went.

Oman's public library system was almost non-existent, but he decided to venture to the university in Muscat and figure out a way to communicate with Alex. The results of her plan would have to dictate his next steps.

On the campus of Muscat University, Hawk attempted to blend in as best as he could. Though the students were overwhelmingly Omani, the faculty members were diverse. Based on the frequent visiting members, an American walking around between buildings wouldn't draw the same kind of attention such an action would anywhere else in the city.

Hawk bought a brief case on his way downtown to serve as a prop while at the school. Though he'd been the recipient of many long glances elsewhere, nobody on campus paid him any attention. Upon arriving at the library, he talked his way past one of the librarians. Hawk claimed that he'd lost his faculty card, convincingly enough that the man at the desk gave him a temporary username and password to log into the computers.

Hawk logged into the joint email account and sent Alex a message, inquiring about how things went. He also asked if she was online at the moment. Passing the time by catching up on current events, he logged back in a half hour later to find that Alex had responded. Her note included a detailed report on her phone conversation with Michaels and how she delivered the information to her reporter friend.

By employing a family friend, Alex explained how she set up a drop on the L train in Chicago as a way of protecting everyone involved. She told Hawk that the reporter reached out to her after receiving the information and promised that he'd write a story within the next couple of days.

Hawk smiled as he read the message. He wrote her back and shared his desire to leave Oman since they'd accomplished what they needed to with Michaels. Since nothing was left for him in Oman, Hawk shared how all he wanted to do was get back west, preferring to wait out Michaels' demise somewhere in Europe.

"I haven't seen a Bollywood movie in ages," he wrote. "And I think I know just the person to watch one with me."

She responded by letting him know that she would contact Blunt and they would establish a rendezvous point.

"Isn't telecommuting amazing?" Hawk wrote in his final message. "I'll look forward to hearing from you."

Hawk walked toward the library exit, thanking the man at the reference desk before leaving. Once the warm air blasted Hawk as he stepped outside, he couldn't help but smile. Fortune had smiled favorably upon the Firestorm team. A prideful and sloppy Michaels had sealed his own fate. In a matter of days, living in hiding would be a distant memory.

However, as Hawk walked back home, he continued to be bothered by the fact that Michaels might still intend to sell weapons to terrorists. Stirring up conflict might still be his way of dodging scrutiny. Hawk considered the possibility that Michaels might dismiss the allegations and claim his victories over terrorist groups as his reason for why the American people should still vote for him. His ability to spin any negative news had become almost legendary. Pundits marveled at the way voters extended grace to a man, who, time and time again, had proven to be anything but trustworthy. But polls showed people felt safe with Michaels in the White House, which proved to be an insurmountable attribute.

Hawk dismissed his concerns as paranoia, choosing to dwell on other topics during his long walk home. Topics such as Blunt's whereabouts, Alex's safety, and the Texas Longhorns' position in the latest Associated Press poll were all welcomed in his mind. As long as Hawk didn't have to consider the possibility that their plan would ultimately fail, he was fine.

Upon arriving at his apartment, Hawk fixed a quick dinner and devoured it in less time than it took to make it. He finished his evening by contemplating his email exchange with Alex on the roof.

Leaning forward on the railing, he watched the lights of Muscat twinkle in the distance. The glow of a city still hard at work illuminated the horizon, reducing the chances of seeing any stars. Though returning to civilization relieved Hawk, he missed the overhead masterpiece provided in the sky soaring over the Al Hajar Mountains. Devoid of light pollution, the canvas that stretched from horizon to horizon had been a pleasure to observe each evening after the thankless task of navigating grumpy customers across challenging terrain. Hawk didn't miss the work, but he couldn't deny how much he enjoyed unwinding beneath the glorious beaming stars each night.

A smile swept across his face as he remembered the pristine beauty while appreciating Muscat's own unique display. But that smile ended abruptly when he felt the blade of a knife jammed dangerously into his back.

"If you want to live, you won't make another move," the man said.

CHAPTER 11

Brighton, England

ALEX GLANCED AT THE CALLER ID on the phone. The word "unknown" lit up the screen, making her anxious about answering it. She quickly considered the consequences of avoiding the call before deciding to pick up.

"Yes," she said.

"Alex, this Mallory Kauffman," the woman on the other end said.

Alex let out a sigh of relief once she recognized the voice of her longtime confidant from NSA.

"I take it you got my message," she said.

"You are good at covering your tracks," Mallory said. "If you ever want to come back—"

"I'm fine where I'm at, thank you. Now, cut the recruiting act and tell me what you found."

Mallory chuckled. "Cool your jets, Alex. I've got

109

good news."

"The suspense is killing me."

"The recording you sent me was—how should I say it—eye opening."

"I didn't send it to you for commentary on its contents," Alex said. "I simply wanted to know if it could be verified."

"In that case, you don't have to worry about a thing. I gave it to one of our digital forensic experts and he verified President Michaels' voice on the recording."

"Why do I get the feeling that a 'but' is coming?"

"Because it is."

"Go ahead. Give me the bad news."

"My expert told me that the voice of the other gentleman on the recording was digitized."

"Meaning . . ."

"Meaning an expert would be able to prove that whoever Michaels was talking to wasn't really the guy he thought he was talking to."

"But would that really matter?"

"Probably not in the court of public opinion, but you know how Michaels and his team are so skilled at spinning a negative into a positive. I would just move forward with caution. There's the possibility that this could come back on the paper and the editor would end up with egg on his face."

"So, essentially you're saying this isn't admissible in court?"

"You're not planning on presenting this in some sort of civil lawsuit, are you?"

"Of course not."

"In that case, this should be fine for throwing a huge wrench in his re-election campaign if it's released soon. But just beware that this isn't a done deal. It still could blow up on you."

"The goal is to expose his deceitful practices—the kind that are endangering the country's safety and destabilizing the Middle East—to the American people so they can decide if they want this man as their leader," Alex said. "That's the goal anyway."

"Well, it's a noble one. Let me know if you need help with anything else."

"Thanks. I'll be in touch."

Alex hung up and opened up her laptop, checking her regular email account from the comfort of her couch. With her feet propped up, she scrolled through the morass of junk mail and social media notifications. She refreshed the inbox and a message from Brian Lawton flashed onto the screen.

Alex's eyes danced over the words as a smile began to spread across her face.

They're running the story tomorrow morning.

She pumped her fist and closed her laptop before

getting ready for bed. She wanted to let Hawk know all about it so he could follow the fallout as it happened in real time. However, the library was closed. She would still have time to let him know in the morning on her way to work, notifying him before news of the scandal went public.

* * *

ALEX DUCKED INTO THE LIBRARY and posted a note for Hawk in their shared draft folder. She continued to work, splashing through the standing water on the sidewalk. Overnight, a rain cloud settled over Brighton and hadn't budged for nearly six hours. In an attempt to avoid getting drenched, she popped up her umbrella and fought to keep it up in a battle with the wind.

At lunchtime, she checked news websites to see if the story on Michaels had broken. Though she was six hours ahead of Chicago, she figured a story that big would've already trickled out. She imagined that news about the president arming terrorists would not only rock the U.S. but also the international community. But she was disappointed to find that it was still business as usual for all the major news outlets.

Maybe they decided to move the story to another day.

Later that afternoon, Alex took a break to check again. Still nothing. Concerned and distracted, she returned to work. For the next hour, she resisted getting online for fear of more disappointment, though she was certain that the story had been delayed for some reason or another. Mallory's warning echoed in her mind, a thought she tried to push away. If Michaels' team got wind of the story *The Chicago Tribune* was planning on running, the president's administration would've attempted to squash it.

Is this really happening?

Alex tried to focus as she convinced herself that Lawton likely ran into some issues verifying his source or some other hangup that prevented the article from running when he said it would. Doing her best to ignore the tornado swirling through her mind, she gave her task her sole attention. But that was short lived when a phone call shattered her concentration.

"This is Alex," she said.

"When was that story supposed to run?" Blunt asked in response.

"This morning. Why?"

"Well, you can forget about it now—the reporter is dead."

"What?" Alex asked, her eyes welling up with tears. "How do you know? When did this happen?"

"I hate delivering news like this," he said. "I'm sorry. I know that Brian Lawton was a good friend of yours. I forgot you were more than acquaintances."

"Tell me what happened," she said, choking back

more tears in an effort to remain composed in the office.

"They're claiming suicide. According to reports, he was drinking at his favorite bar after work last night and went home and jumped off the balcony of his high-rise apartment. The editor must've pulled the story when he heard about Lawton's death—and I doubt the article will run at all now."

"This was all my fault."

"No, it wasn't," Blunt said. "Some of Michaels' goons are the ones who did this. Your friend was simply doing his job. I'm sure you warned him about the danger, didn't you?"

"Yes, but—"

"But that was his choice. Everyone covering this administration knows what Michaels is capable of. His death was for a noble cause."

"And now I'm afraid it will be for nothing."

"Alex, that's not like you to give up so easily," Blunt said. "The Alex I know is tenacious and determined. You wouldn't take something like this sitting down."

"It's just too many people are dying because of decisions I've made—people who I consider my friends."

"This should make you more focused on figuring out a way to take Michaels down. None of us are going to get our lives back until that bastard is out of office—and preferably dead."

"I just don't know if I can go on like this," she said. "So much senseless loss."

"There's gonna be a helluva lot more of it if we don't do something. Today you cry for your friend; tomorrow you might weep for thousands who die senselessly at the hands of some terrorists armed and emboldened by Michaels. We can't let our individual pain stop us from seeing this same kind of pain spread exponentially across this country. If we don't do something, who will?"

Alex sniffled and dried the outer corners of her eyes. She took a deep breath and exhaled slowly.

"You're right," she said. "I can grieve later."

"And you will, but right now we need another plan of attack to get Michaels on his heels."

"What do you suggest?"

"Given how Michaels has crushed stories by murdering journalists in the past, I only see one real option—Wikileaks."

"I was afraid you were going to say that," Alex said. "That's only going to be more difficult in convincing the American people that what the audio captured Michaels doing really happened."

"Don't underestimate the American people. They can be a fiercely loyal group, but when they feel betrayed, watch out. Hopefully, Michaels will bear the brunt of their wrath."

"We can only hope," Alex said. "I'll contact Wik-ileaks as soon as I get off work."

CHAPTER 12

Muscat, Oman

HAWK REMAINED FROZEN, unsure if the blade that had already pierced his shirt would continue to slide into his back. He considered turning around quickly to incite a fight, but he knew what he was up against. With just one wrong move, Hawk understood the consequences would be severe if not fatal.

Hawk stumbled forward as the man gave him a firm push in his back.

"You weren't scared I was gonna kill you?" the man said.

Hawk turned around to look Ray Green in the eyes. With the knife at his side, Ray flashed a wide grin.

"Well, I wasn't sure of anything based on the treatment your boss gave me a couple of days ago," Hawk said, glancing at the blade in Ray's hand.

Ray closed the knife and slid it into his pocket.

"That's Ackerman's way of telling you that he likes you," Ray said with a wink. "Seriously, he was just wanting to test you and see your range of skills."

"There are other ways of doing that besides sending an assassin after a prospective employee."

Ray shrugged. "It's a proven method for Ackerman. He's lost some good men using that tactic—but if he does, he always gains a better one."

Hawk shook his head. "That's a twisted way of looking at it."

"Perhaps, but you can't argue with the results."

Hawk walked to the edge of the railing surrounding the balcony and looked down at the street below.

"How did you find me, Ray?"

"It's Muscat, Hawk. And you're an expat. It's difficult for people like us to hide in a city like this. On top of that, I'm very well connected. And anyone that doesn't look like they belong here becomes the talk of the neighborhood. You'd have to damn near be a ghost to disappear in this city."

"Look, I owe you an apology," Hawk said.

"About the money?" Ray asked.

Hawk nodded.

Ray waved dismissively. "Don't worry about it, man. I understand why you'd be wary of coming by. And I knew you needed it. No harm, no foul."

"I was afraid I was in danger—and I didn't know

where your loyalties rested. At one time, we weren't exactly the best of friends."

"Water under the bridge as far as I'm concerned."

Hawk paced around, glancing between the cityscape and Ray.

"So, why are you really here?"

"Ackerman wants to offer you a job."

"Seriously? After all that I did to his men?"

"Well, you didn't kill any of them, which will endear you to most of the guys. That much I know for a fact. Honestly, Ackerman was impressed that you could've killed them if you wanted to—but you chose not to. You had the power and exercised it judiciously. And that's exactly the kind of man he wants for an upcoming operation we have."

"What kind of operation?"

"I can't tell you that just yet. Ackerman is the one who decides what and when to release information about upcoming missions. All I can really tell you is that the money is very good."

"I'd need a dollar figure on that amount," Hawk said. "We might have differing opinions on what constitutes good money."

"It's enough to get you out of this dump."

Hawk chuckled. "If you think this is a dump, you should've seen where I lived when I was working as a tour guide in Al Hajar. This place is a virtual palace in comparison."

"If it's specifics you want, I'll give them to you— a two-day mission, fifty thousand a day."

"A hundred G's? This must be some kind of assignment."

Ray shrugged. "I'm sure Ackerman will be happy to give you all the details if you're still interested and want to come down to the office and tell him personally that you're going to accept."

"You can let him know that I'll plan on making my way down there tomorrow around noon."

"I know he'll be very pleased," Ray said. "Now, you might want to shore up your defenses around this place. If I can get through here so easily, I'm sure there will be others to follow."

"Some of Ackerman's men?"

"No," Ray said. "I'm talking about street rats— you know, those kids who get a kick out of stealing stuff from people without fear of any real retribution."

"Good thing I've got nothing here for now."

"When you do acquire some essentials, they'll pick you clean if you're not careful. So, that's my word of warning."

"I'll be careful," Hawk said. "I'll promise to do a perimeter assessment tonight if it'll make you feel better."

"It'll make me feel a lot better. Ciao."

Hawk settled into one of the wooden chairs atop the balcony and wondered what he'd just gotten himself into. He was hoping it would be enough to stop the sale of the weapons to Al Hasib. Deep down he also hoped to get a crack at the terrorist outfit that had wreaked havoc all across the Middle East, the aftermath drifting onto the shores of Washington, D.C.

He settled into his chair and stared at the twinkling lights in the city below as he contemplated how he should proceed. Telling Alex was a must, but such a decision would lead to a protest, albeit a mild one. He needed to be ready with an explanation for why such a mission was necessary.

And he was more than ready. Ray had been evasive about the meeting, but he didn't need to be. Hawk already knew what it was that Ackerman was going to ask him to do.

CHAPTER 13

Washington, D.C.

MICHAELS GRIPPED THE LECTERN, knuckles whitening as he surveyed the room packed with journalists. Flash bulbs exploded as he looked down at his notes and prepared to speak. Under the circumstances, the last place he wanted to be was standing at a press conference and answering questions from a pack of media members, who looked as though they were frothing at the mouth to tear into him.

Damn Wikipedia.

The bombshell dropped by the website just a few hours earlier contained a recording of him engaged in a conversation with someone named "Ollie." Several news agencies proffered forth a wide range of possibilities, but no one could pin down the voice of the speaker without a wide margin of error.

"Today, I stand before you ashamed," Michaels

began. "Ashamed that we live in a society where news gets reported before it gets verified. Ashamed that we seek to take down our political opponents with a public display of grandeur while privately entering into collegial relationships that extend far beyond partisan boundaries. Ashamed that good theater trumps the truth. And today, I'm here to speak with you in order to set the record straight.

"The United States isn't interested in selling weapons to terrorists or any other rogue factions living among sovereign states. That's not what this country is about nor is it what we do. And any reports suggesting otherwise are patently false.

"The phone call you heard me on was little more than a deceptive trick to make me sound as I was attempting to do the thing I was accused of doing. But the reality is that the voice has been altered and digitally enhanced. Our forensics experts have done an incredible job in determining that the voice that was spliced onto the audio file with mine is not talking about the same thing. In essence, someone recorded my voice and manipulated my answers in small nuggets to make me sound as if I was talking about selling weapons to a terrorist group.

"Not only was that wrong—it was also criminal. And I can promise you that whoever compiled that recording will be severely punished once they are caught.

"At this time, the perpetrators behind this heinous act have yet to be identified. I'm not prepared to answer any questions on the topic, which will be addressed next week at a briefing with my spokesperson. In the meantime, I suggest that you do your due diligence as part of the free press and dig deep into the players behind this stunt. The timing appears suspect at best, launching this into the public sphere with no accountability just weeks before the election. Whoever these people are that want to smear my name among the American people are also smearing democracy. And I won't stand for it—and neither should you."

Michaels released his grip and stepped down from the podium. The gaggle of journalists present shouted questions at him, questions that demanded an answer. He wanted to stop and defend himself. To Michaels, this was a vicious attempt at a political takedown, directed by someone with inside knowledge of what he was doing. If he were in any other position, he would've been afraid of being exposed. But as president, he knew he could swing the full weight of the law to his side and eviscerate the people behind this virtual coup.

"How'd I do?" Michaels asked Kriegel after rejoining behind the closed doors of the Oval Office.

"You really sold it," Kriegel said.

Michaels narrowed his eyes. "What was there to *sell*? I was only sharing the truth. This wasn't some spin job."

"You can bullshit the American people, but you can't bullshit me. I know what's going on."

"What's going on is someone is trying to prematurely end my place in office through nefarious means. I don't have time to ward off every whisper of treason that appears in *The Post* or *The Times* or *The Tribune*. These claims are patently false, designed to cast me in the poorest of light among the American people."

"So, that phone call really was cobbled together by someone? I heard what you said for myself when you answered. I was standing right there. Please tell me you weren't simply fooled by the caller. Please tell me you were discussing anything else but what it sounded like you were talking about."

Michaels pounded his fist on his desk.

"I swear to God, David, if you keep this up, you might be looking for a new job before I will."

"As much as I like this job, it isn't everything to me. What's more important is that I know everything I'm getting myself into. At least tell me the truth so I can make my own decisions about whether I want to stay or go."

"Perhaps you should stop asking questions and do your job. Find out who's trying to make a run at me, and let's cut them off at the knees so you and I won't have to worry."

Kriegel nodded. "You really think this is a political opponent?"

"Why wouldn't it be? Probably one of those super pacs from the coal industry. They will do anything to hold onto their fleeting power."

Kriegel nervously clicked his pen. "What if it's someone else trying to take you down for other reasons?"

"What do you mean?"

"What if this has nothing to do with politics per se and everything to do with getting you out of office?"

"Aren't those things two in the same?"

"Yes, but suppose someone who has a strong reason to see you gone used this moment as a diversion. What if it's someone you would never even consider right now?"

Michaels leaned back in his chair and spun around to face the window. He stared pensively outside for a moment before responding.

"There's only one person who would not only have the resources to pull this off but would also have the gall to make a run at me."

"And who would that be?"

"The one and only Brady Hawk."

CHAPTER 14

Brighton, England

ALEX SLAMMED HER LAPTOP closed and stood up abruptly, knocking her chair backward with a kick. She growled as she paced around her kitchen. Despite her hatred for Michaels, she begrudgingly had to admit that he put on quite a show during the press conference, deflecting and redirecting the accusations that hadn't even had time to rise to the top of trending subjects on social media. Michaels was a master at getting out in front of public relations nightmares—and she loathed him for it.

"The Teflon Man," she muttered. "Is there anything that will ever stick to you?"

With Michaels swatting down her plan with a press conference, he endured no more than a few hours of scrutiny before the entire narrative was turned on its head. Instead of journalists getting their hands dirty and digging into why Michaels would be engaged in such a conversation in the first place—real or contrived—every reporter from New York to L.A. would be doing the president's dirty work for him. All political rivals would have their closets opened, where past sins would be paraded out into the open. Those reports would likely dominate the media's offering to the public in the coming days, while Michaels reaps the benefit of appearing like a victim. Alex had underestimated the president's political genius once again.

She dialed Mallory's number.

"I thought I might be hearing from you," Mallory said once she answered the phone.

"I swear he's made of Teflon," Alex said. "I'm going to have to wait four more years to get my life back, if I can stay hidden that long. Meanwhile, he continues his mission of ruining the country all for his personal gain."

"That's kind of what most presidents do these days. It's not like he's all that unique in that department."

"Well, I'm tired of it. This is absolutely ridiculous. He made a mockery of the press today with that stunt he pulled. Now all of a sudden he's the victim of some politically-minded attack, distracting the American people from what they really need to know about their leader."

"I'm sure something will come out soon enough."

"But what? And when? It'll probably be too late. In a few weeks, voters will hit the reset button with him and give him another four years. I don't see that changing unless something drastic occurs."

"Hmmm," Mallory said before a long pregnant pause.

"What is it?"

"Just promise me you won't do anything rash, will you? I don't want to have to testify against you if called."

Alex chuckled. "I wouldn't give him the pleasure of stooping to his level. I'm going to stay above the fray. I just don't know what to do to bring him down."

"From a political perspective, I don't think there's much you can do. He has insulated himself well. Now, I'm not advocating any of this, but if you really want to put a dent in his political aspirations, you need to force him into a corner so he makes a mistake. And then you need to be there to document it in a way that he can't spin it against you."

"I've tried that before, believe me. But he always manages to somehow pull his Houdini act and vanish when it comes time to suffer the consequences."

"Then you need to do a better job of it. Put his back against the wall and push. He's still human. He'll cave at some point. But you're probably not going to be able to do that on your own. You're going to need some help."

"Are you volunteering?" Alex asked.

Mallory sighed. "Not in the least. I work at the NSA, remember? But I will be rooting for you to bring the truth to light. Good luck."

Alex hung up and circled the kitchen several times before adding the living room to her route.

Think, Alex. Think. There has to be some way.

When an idea finally struck her, she rushed over to her computer and opened it up. Pounding on the keyboard, she hacked into several offshore bank accounts in search of a name.

Less than an hour later, she'd found what she was looking for.

"There you are," she said with a wry smile. "And my, what a large number. We'll have to do something about that, won't we."

CHAPTER 15

Muscat, Oman

THE GUARD AT THE GATE flinched when he saw Hawk. With his hands held in the air in a posture of surrender, Hawk eyed the guard closely, studying his neck. A large red mark on the man's neck served as a reminder of Hawk's siege from just a few days earlier. The guard's nostrils flared as he glanced at Hawk before calling the main office.

"I'm not here to hurt anybody," Hawk said.

The man exited the guardhouse and shoved Hawk in his back, pushing him toward the offices.

"Is that really necessary?" Hawk asked.

"Was it really necessary to storm this compound and shoot a bunch of fellow former soldiers?"

"Sometimes when you're auditioning for a job—"

"That was no audition," the guard said. "That was an assault, and you know it. But I've heard all about you, Mr. Pearl."

"Good things, I hope."

"Just shut up and walk. I don't really want to hear the sound of your voice."

"Don't be so quick to judge," Hawk said. "We're on the same team now. We're gonna be working together."

"Working together, my ass."

"That's what the scuttlebutt around the water cooler is."

"You better hope that Ackerman isn't planning on paying you back."

Hawk shook his head and kept walking until they reached the office entrance. The guard nodded toward the door, and Hawk opened it before receiving one final jab in the back from the guard's rifle.

"Do you treat all your fellow co-workers like this?" Hawk asked as he stumbled forward.

"Only the ones who shoot me in the neck. Now sit down and wait for Mr. Ackerman."

Hawk settled into a chair as instructed and watched the guard march back to his post, kicking rocks along the way.

"That one's got a temper on him, doesn't he?" Hawk quipped to the man sitting behind the receptionist's desk.

"Can't say that I blame him for how he feels."

"You should be on my side," Hawk said. "I didn't even shoot you."

The man ignored Hawk's comment.

"Let me see if Mr. Ackerman is available."

He then picked up the phone and dialed a number. "He'll be down in just a moment."

Less than a minute later, Ackerman galloped down the steps and clasped his hands together upon seeing Hawk.

"Chuck, I told you we'd find something for you to do here," Ackerman said.

"You didn't have to try and kill me to see if I was suited for the position," Hawk countered.

"Oh, yes, I did. That's kind of a rite of passage around here. Or more like a sign that you have what it takes."

"For those who don't have what it takes?"

"We help usher them into retirement sooner, if you catch my drift."

Hawk nodded. "It's a brutal business you run."

"It's a brutal world out there. And our clients expect to be kept safe. We can't very well do that with subpar guards, can we?"

"I suppose not," Hawk said.

"Say, Chuck, why don't you join me upstairs in my office so we can finish going over the details of your assignment?"

Hawk followed Ackerman up the steps and into his office where the two men settled into plush chairs in a seating area in the corner of the room.

"These chairs are far more comfortable than anything you'll find out in the field," Hawk said as he squeezed the arms. "You're going to make your men soft by sitting in these things."

"I'm anything but soft on the people who are seated in front of me, no matter how cushy the chairs are," Ackerman said.

"So, let's get down to business," Hawk said, rubbing his hands together and leaning forward. "Ray tells me that you've got a pretty big job for me."

"Did he tell you the pay?"

Hawk nodded. "That's a hefty payout. Kind of hard to turn down."

"That was what I was hoping for anyway. So, now that I've got you here, I need to fill you in on all the details."

"Please do."

"In two days from now, you're going to Khabas, a small port city in the northern tip of Oman where you'll handle an exchange for me."

"What type of exchange?"

Ackerman pursed his lips and turned to look pensively out of the window before refocusing his gaze on Hawk.

"It's probably best that you didn't know, at least for your own sake," Ackerman said.

"Plausible deniability?" Hawk asked.

"Something like that. It's just a simple exchange. You'll have some cargo that they'll want to inspect. You allow them to check it out. They will give you the money and it's over. They'll haul off anything they want to keep and load it onto their boat and you'll never see one another again. It's that easy."

"Doesn't sound too difficult. But do you really need someone of my caliber to handle such a simple operation?"

"I can't have any of my guys getting fingered for this if something were to go awry," Ackerman said. "I usually hire independent contractors like yourself to take care of these transactions. It's better for everyone involved. You get a big payday and—"

"And you avoid getting tied to a potential scandal in case everything goes sideways."

"That's the idea. However, you won't be alone. I'll be sending a small team of men to help provide you with cover in case they attempt to get away without paying or if they decide to harm you in any way."

"That's comforting," Hawk said.

"That's the gig—take it or leave it. But I don't think you're in a position to leave it, are you? If you're stealing from your friends, you might not want to pass up this offer, the likes of which you may never see again."

"I think I can handle this. Who will I be meeting with at the exchange?" Hawk asked.

"You don't need to worry about that right now," Ackerman said. "One of their representatives from the organization will be there to guide you through the whole thing. Names aren't so important."

"Yeah, the whole the-less-you-know deal."

"Exactly. So are you on board now?"

"A hundred percent."

"Now one more thing before you leave," Ackerman said.

"What is it?"

"You'll know who these guys are when you see them, but no hero stuff, okay? Make the exchange and get out. If you do that, everything will be fine. No need to upset the apple cart, understand?"

Hawk nodded. "Got it."

"Good. Now, let's get you downstairs to fill out some paperwork so you can get paid. Half up front, half upon completion."

An hour later, Hawk walked across the compound and exited the grounds. The guard sneered at Hawk as he left. He had agreed to work for Ackerman, but he felt there was something else at play, something he just couldn't put his finger on—and he didn't have much time to figure it out.

CHAPTER 16

Nuremberg, Germany

SINCE MICHAELS' INTENTIONS became clear regarding the Firestorm team, J.D. Blunt had spent his time roaming about Europe at various hideouts. Relying on his ability to remain hidden in plain sight, he rented expensive villas that would've presented a challenge to conquer for even the best operatives the U.S. possessed. He'd only come out of hiding to discuss some issues with Alex, choosing a secluded lifestyle for the purposes of self-preservation.

But Blunt received a message from General Van Fortner that forced him to venture out again into public, albeit in a private place.

Blunt eased into his seat in a back corner of the Zwei Sinn restaurant, one of his favorites in Nuremburg. Located less than an hour from where he was staying, the dining establishment was somewhat close to Fortner, who was serving a stint at the U.S. Army base in Hohenfels. Fortner had been adamant that their conversation needed to be had in person, if anything for protection against Michaels.

Blunt enjoyed a glass of wine while waiting for Fortner. The pair had developed a closer bond in recent years due to the challenging climate foisted upon them by Michaels' administration. Looking out for one another was imperative for surviving in that environment.

Fortner arrived five minutes late and apologized for his tardiness.

"I owe you more than you know," Blunt said. "If it weren't for you, I'd probably be buried somewhere in an unmarked grave by this point. I'm happy to wait five minutes for you."

"You're too kind, J.D."

"Just being honest. I am very sincere in my gratitude for how you've helped the Firestorm team."

"I'm hoping that I can be of help again tonight," Fortner said.

"So, that's what this is about?"

"It's not a big message, but it's one I needed to deliver because I feel like something is going on that you might want to know about. I just couldn't risk sending this electronically. I'm sure it would've been intercepted by someone."

"That was wise," Blunt said before taking a long pull on his glass.

"Well, what I'm about to tell you is highly classified, so please use the utmost discretion when discussing this with any members of your team."

"We have a protocol in place to handle sensitive matters, so you don't need to worry about that."

"All right. Since that's out of the way, here's what you need to know. A group of Rangers have been deployed to the northern tip of Oman, just outside Khasab. Now, from the intel I've read in the past, that area is a secret rendezvous point for Al Hasib. It's where they handle the majority of their weapons deals."

"Sounds interesting," Blunt said. "What's this have to do with my team?"

"In the briefing I read, they are going not to obliterate Al Hasib but to arrest an American operative who's been on the lam for nearly a year. I didn't have access to the full document, but from what I read it sounded a lot like Hawk."

"You think someone is trying to set him up right now?"

Fortner nodded. "Michaels is desperate to prove he's going to be the candidate who keeps Americans the most secure. If he can bring home a supposed traitor trying to deal weapons to Al Hasib just a few weeks before the election, that's a huge political win for him."

"Are you sure it isn't some other mercenary? I mean, why Hawk?"

"Former Navy Seal who is highly trained and labeled as very dangerous. Who does that sound like to you?"

"That could be any one of a dozen men."

"And where is Hawk now?"

"I really shouldn't say."

Fortner cocked his head to one side and arched his eyebrows.

"Okay," Blunt relented. "He's in Oman."

"They're setting him up, J.D."

"Hawk's too smart for that. He'd smell that coming from a mile away."

"What if he has no choice?"

Blunt sighed. "There's not much I could do about it right now. Alex is the one who has contact with him. I have to relay all my messages through her."

"Then call her tonight. Hawk's future might depend on it."

"I'll see what I can do."

"Take this seriously, J.D. You know Michaels will relish the opportunity to put him away for good, effectively shutting you down. Even if you stay in hiding the rest of your life, he won't care as long as you can't touch him."

"I appreciate you letting me know about this, I really do. I wish we knew further in advance."

"Me too," Fortner said as he picked up the menu and began studying it. "Metoo."

* * *

WHEN BLUNT RETURNED to his house of the week, he called Alex to see if she could get the message to Hawk.

"Michaels is planning on doing what?" she asked.

"When I spoke with Fortner tonight, he seems to be under the impression that this is all one big setup."

"Hawk has been trying to get a job through one of his former Navy Seal buddies. Surely he wouldn't let Hawk twist in the wind."

"Throw enough money at people and they'll sell out their own mothers if it came down to it," Blunt said. "You've been around long enough to know that."

"I guess you're right, but that's what makes this all the more depressing."

"What are you talking about?"

"I can leave a message for him, but I never know when he's going to check it. For all we know, he could already be on his mission now."

"You've gotta try, Alex."

"I can't do anything until the morning when the library opens. I've been very careful about when and where and how I utilize the email account that he set up for us. If I opened it now from my apartment, it could set off alarm bells somewhere. And that's the last thing we need right now."

"Just send the message in the morning and pray it gets to him in time. Otherwise, he'll be all on his own when he's blindsided."

Blunt hung up and said a little prayer of his own. Even Hawk would need a little extra help on this mission.

CHAPTER 17

Muscat, Oman

LATER THAT EVENING, Hawk hustled near the Fortress Security compound. Quickly scaling the wall using a grappling hook, he climbed over and eased his way down. The grounds were well lit but relatively quiet. Hawk had only seen two guards patrolling the area, though most of the time they were seated against the wall smoking cigars.

Unlike last time, Hawk didn't want a soul to know he was there. If he was going to find out the real goal for this mission, he needed to slip into Ackerman's office without the boss ever knowing what happened.

While the front door was the most direct route, Hawk had observed a utility shed that had a rollup garage door and connected to the inside of the office building. And the door was rolled up, almost serving as an open invitation for Hawk. He decided to risk it; entering any other way would be foolish.

Hawk watched the two guards reclining against the wall with plumes of smoke rising above them. Laughing as they swapped stories, Hawk charged ahead with his plan to access the main facility. The door to the inside was unlocked and Hawk prepared to go inside.

I hope the security system is armed. Where's Alex when I really need her?

Hawk held his breath as he turned the doorknob and opened the door. He winced as he stepped inside, hoping that he wouldn't hear a dreaded alarm sounding. Instead, complete silence.

Hawk hustled up the stairs to Ackerman's office and activated the flashlight on his phone. He rifled through some papers on his desk in search of the mission files. Upon locating a familiar folder, Hawk scanned the pages until he recognized some of the mission details that Ackerman had already related to him—weapons exchange, port near Khabas, terrorist organization. Hawk stopped and went back and read the name of the terrorist group again.

Al Hasib. Al Hasib? Michaels is going to sell weapons to Al Hasib?

Hawk continued reading and noted that most of the weapons were going to be sabotaged. The few the

Al Hasib agents would try out at the exchange would work—but the rest of the guns and grenade launchers would fail in battle.

Michaels knows how to make an enemy for life, doesn't he?

Hawk continued reading and learned that the plot was a complete ruse, one designed to give Michaels a big political win. If he were to bag one of the biggest terrorists since Osama bin Laden, it would do wonders for Michaels' poll numbers, rendering the upcoming election little more than a foregone conclusion.

For a moment, Hawk contemplated throwing a wrench in Michaels' plan. Maybe Hawk could hunt down and kill Fazil, though that too would create a win for Michaels. Hawk considered warning Al Hasib about the weapons at the exchange. Such a move would be bold, but Hawk concluded it'd just make him a common enemy, lumped in with the rest of the American government, not to mention they might kill him on the spot. There had to be something he could do, but he would have to consider it later. He poked his head high up enough to see the two guards had left their spot and were presumably patrolling the grounds again.

Hawk returned the scattered files to the place where he'd discovered them and crept out of the room. Once downstairs, Hawk eased back outside, using the utility doorway.

As he rounded the corner, he heard plodding footfalls approaching his direction. He crouched low and hoped they would veer in a different direction. Instead, the guard marched straight toward him.

Hawk stayed low, leaping up just as the man walked by. Hawk pistol whipped him, sending him staggering against the wall. He hit his head and collapsed to the ground without ever making eye contact with Hawk.

Good night, little buddy. I hope you don't remember a thing.

Hawk hustled down the street and headed straight for Ray's apartment.

* * *

"DO YOU EVER SLEEP?" Ray said with a growl as he opened the door. "Why couldn't you have just broken in like last time? It's two o'clock in the morning."

Hawk ignored the complaint, pushing his way past Ray.

"What's the hurry?" Ray said again before shutting the door.

"Do you know what's going on with this exchange?" Hawk asked.

Ray nodded. "Yeah, we're gonna screw over those Al Hasib thugs."

"Not screw them over," Hawk said. "You're going to infuriate them. I don't really understand the thinking behind this. Why would our government sanction this?"

"They didn't just sanction it—they ordered it. Look, I don't understand everything our government does. I just do what I'm told. I'm a soldier."

"A soldier without a conscience?"

"Hey, now. You have no moral high ground here. Your sole reason for getting involved is a hundred G's, am I not right?"

"It's not like that."

"Then what's it like, Hawk? From where I stand, you're a mercenary, just like me. Money talks—period. You could get out if you wanted to. Nothing's stopping you."

"I can't leave now. Ackerman would just replace me, and I can't let this deal go down. The blowback will be fierce and swift. Michaels has no idea what he's doing."

"Like I said, I just follow orders."

"Bullshit," Hawk said as he narrowed his eyes. "I've seen you defy orders before."

Ray shrugged. "So, what do you want to do about it? Kill some Al Hasib terrorists as a way of sending Michaels a message? He might even appreciate that and throw a parade for us."

"No, that's not what I was thinking at all. Maybe we could give them what they came to buy in the first place."

"Are you insane? Speaking of soldiers without a conscience—they'll kill thousands of innocent people if we arm them with properly functioning weapons."

"Look, we could put tracking devices in the weapons and hunt them down before they had a chance to use them. Ultimately, this is all a big setup to capture Karif Fazil so Michaels can assure himself another four-year term. We can't let that happen."

"*You* can't let that happen," Ray said. "Meet the new boss, same as the old one. The political parties are one and the same in my book."

"Would you help me smoke out Al Hasib and take them down if I placed a tracking device in the weapons shipment?"

"I guess so. Not sure how we'd have the fire-power to do that."

"I have some friends who can help. But I just need to know you're on board with this plan. I can't do this alone."

"Okay," Ray said. "I'll help. However, you have to answer one question for me. How do you think this is going to help *you*?"

"If I capture Fazil without the help of U.S. military forces, I'll return to the U.S. a hero. Michaels won't be able to touch me then."

"But Michaels still gets another four years. Doesn't seem like you've thought this through."

"There's another way to deal with Michaels. My goal is two-fold and begins and ends with him not getting what he wants."

"You're ambitious—I'll give you that."

"Just be ready. Now, I need to use your computer to send my people a message."

Hawk logged on and wrote a message to Alex, leaving it in the draft folder of their joint account. He informed her that he'd discovered the real intent behind the weapon exchange and his new plan. He also encouraged her to watch over satellite in case something went wrong, giving her the coordinates and time for the rendezvous. He finished by explaining that he was going dark and he'd reconnect after everything went down.

When he finished, Hawk announced he was going back to his apartment for the night and would see Ray at the compound in the morning.

"We've got a long day ahead of us tomorrow," Hawk said. "Get some good sleep."

"I was trying until someone stormed into my apartment in the middle of the night," Ray said.

Hawk patted Ray on the shoulder. "I was wrong to think ill of you. You're a good friend."

"I won't be so kind if you make me miss out on sleep again."

Hawk smiled and said goodnight. As he exited

Ray's place, he had a sense of hope for the first time in months. He was going to take down two enemies almost at once.

* * *

RAY WAITED TEN MINUTES after Hawk left to be sure that his friend wasn't lurking outside. If he heard any of the conversation that was about to happen, Ray knew he'd likely be killed.

He dialed Ackerman's number.

"Couldn't this have waited until the morning, Ray?" Ackerman said with a growl when he answered.

"Your friend, *Mr. Pearl*, just stopped by to see me."

"He still has no clue, does he?"

"Nope. And he took the bait. He broke in and read the file you left on your desk about tomorrow's operation."

"And?" Ackerman asked.

"And he wants to plant a tracking device on the weapons shipment. He wants to be a hero and thinks that will be a way for him to march back to Washington and get his life back."

"Just play it cool with him. I don't want him getting suspicious, even for a minute. The more control he thinks he's in, the better. This whole operation began because Michaels wanted those weapons in the hands of Al Hasib. The more terror in the region, the better. But he couldn't pass up the opportunity to set up Hawk either. It's petty but I understand given the past history between them. Michaels can eliminate a foe and get a boost in ratings at the same time for capturing a traitor abroad. And then he'll swoop in and snag Karif Fazil just a few days before the election to seal the deal."

"We know where Fazil is hiding out?"

"From what I understand, we've been watching his location for months. All Michaels has to do is say the word."

"Just be forewarned that Hawk is a force to be reckoned with when he wants to be. And if he wants to turn this thing on its head, he just might pull it off."

"You're the one who will need to heed your own warning. You keep him under control. After all, you're the one who's going to deliver him personally to Michaels."

"Lucky me."

"Lucky you, indeed," Ackerman said. "I'm going to give you the rest of the money I'd promised Hawk—excuse me, Mr. Pearl—for completing the exchange."

"Can't complain about that."

CHAPTER 18

Brighton, England

ALEX WOKE UP EARLY to make sure she was the first one in the Brighton library when it opened. She tried to act calm when the woman jangling a large set of keys sauntered toward the door and unlocked it. But Alex couldn't help herself, nearly bowling over the woman to get to the bank of computers.

Alex settled into a seat and banged out her login credentials to gain access. Moments later, she read Hawk's note. With each sentence, her despair increased. She felt sorry for him at first, a noble man who'd been betrayed by one of his friends. Hawk's confidence—the kind of chutzpah that believed he could capture Karif Fazil—never ceased to amaze her. But from what she knew based on what Hawk understood, Alex realized he was walking right into a trap.

That sonofabitch Michaels is killing two birds with one stone.

Alex threw her head back and exhaled. With a deep breath, she tried to think of a way that would help her get a message to Hawk. He had no cell phone and, even if he did have one, he likely wouldn't have any cell coverage. She invited a moment of levity to the situation and considered hiring a skywriter to deliver a message in the most non-discreet sort of ways.

He'd get a kick out of that.

But the reality was Alex had no way of alerting Hawk to the fact that he was driving straight into a trap. In Hawk's moment of weakness, he acted desperately, and someone was there who knew him and took advantage of the situation.

Alex logged out of the system and trudged to her office at Lloyd's Bank. She didn't figure anything would get her mind off the impending doom about to befall Hawk—and she was right. For most of the day, she labored with a sense of dread. She skipped lunch and called Blunt to deliver the news.

"There's no way you can work some of your magic to tell him what's going down?" Blunt asked.

"I've considered everything, but I can't get over the challenge of communicating with him when we have no direct access. It's never been a serious problem until now. And if there had been a safer way for us to stay in touch, I'm sure we would've tried it. But there wasn't. And now there's no way for me to let him know anything. I even thought about hiring a sky-writer for about a minute."

"You have thought of everything, haven't you?" he asked with a half-hearted laugh.

"Unfortunately, none of those ideas will get us any message to Hawk. I'm afraid he's on his own."

"I'll send you the security codes you need to log into the NSA's satellites?"

"Thanks. I appreciate it, though I'm not too fond about the idea of watching him get carted off to prison by a bunch of Army Rangers. He saved some of their lives not that long ago."

"Nobody in Washington cares about that," Blunt said. "All the career military personnel at the Pentagon care about is ticking off the box that they accomplished a mission successfully so they can earn the next promotion. With a little bit of luck, they might even catch the president's eye and land on a powerful committee. Those people are far too removed from the battlefield to remember—or even care—about life in the trenches and how important morale and camaraderie is to soldiers in battle. They just go follow the next directive and don't ask any questions. It's easier that way."

"All that to say that Hawk's past interactions with the Rangers won't buy him anything?"

"They might buy him a pillow to lay his head on

and some gentler treatment while they transport him home," Blunt said. "But other than that, not much."

"So, Hawk is screwed."

"Pretty much," Blunt said. "And if Michaels would go to such lengths to make sure that this mission is carried out, you can bet that he's gunning for us next."

"This is not how I want to live," Alex said.

"Me either. But right now we're not in the position to be making any demands. We're alive and free for the moment. And that means we have a fighting chance."

"Wish we could say the same for Hawk."

"Don't give up on him yet," Blunt said. "You know how resourceful he can be. And you too. Maybe you'll think of something between now and the time he meets with Al Hasib."

"I don't know if I can. I'm too depressed to get creative."

"Well, snap out of it because Hawk needs you. If there was something I could do about it, I would."

"Okay, I'll try to focus for Hawk's sake."

"Do it for yourself too. Dwelling on the negative will never get you anywhere."

Alex hung up and returned to her office, counting down the hours until she could leave work and contemplate how she might be able to help Hawk.

* * *

THIRTY MINUTES BEFORE SHE was supposed to leave work, Alex bolted for the door. She called her supervisor and complained about stomach cramps, which was an excuse that men rarely questioned. On her way home from work, she purchased a pair of computer monitors to hook up to her desktop. She planned to utilize all the resources she could to figure out a way to help Hawk in what she considered was a final stand against Michaels.

By the time she arrived at her apartment, she had less than three hours before the deal was supposed to happen. With Oman being three time zones ahead of her in Brighton, she already felt the pressure. Hawk had relayed in his last message that the meeting was scheduled to take place at 11 p.m. local time in Khabas.

Alex configured the monitors with her desktop before firing up her laptop as well. She took fifteen minutes using Blunt's codes to hack into the NSA's satellites to zoom in on the coordinates Hawk had given her. At the moment, there didn't appear to be much activity in the area. The port appeared relatively quiet with only a fishing vessel docked. She took note of the oddly-shaped lifeboat that was secured just off the top deck.

"That looks like a cigarette boat," she said to

herself. "This has to be the ship Al Hasib is going to sail away in with the weapons because that lifeboat is plan B. It's not going to save anyone but the person driving away in it with some of the goods."

Dropping a pin on the harbor, she panned back and searched the rest of the area. She was hoping to spot Hawk well in advance and pray that an idea struck her so she could communicate with him. But he wasn't anywhere to be found.

However, she wasted no time in identifying a three-truck military convoy humming across the desert toward Khabas.

There they are, on their way to arrest one of their own citizens who is truly on their side. Disgraceful.

She made note of the position for the trio of vehicles, which were about a half hour out from the port. Pulling the field of view back again, she searched for Hawk's transport truck. Still nothing.

Alex still had some work to do with the information she'd recently collected from Oliver Ackerman. Though the possibility that none of what she was about to do would matter in a couple of hours, she had to try. Her fingers flew across the keyboard as her strokes were focused and intentional. She knew what she was doing.

He's going to hate this, but I don't care.

When she finished, Alex glanced back up at the

screen and noticed that the Rangers were almost to the port. Meanwhile, two trucks had stopped near the meeting point, parking on the top of a ridge. From that vantage point, the drivers could likely see everything down to the water.

That has to be where Hawk is.

But she quickly realized he couldn't see the U.S. military vehicles that had taken up a position behind a nearby warehouse, using it as cover. When Alex panned back, she could see all the players involved. From what she could tell, the Rangers were in prime position to intercept Hawk if he ventured down to sell the weapons. But she wasn't sure about the terrorists. Al Hasib agents moved cautiously around the docks. They didn't act suspiciously, but they appeared more business-like than a normal crew of a fishing vessel docked would be. The merriment and joking that would have accompanied crew members at a port with a chance to get their feet on dry ground was gone. Instead, men hustled around the docks, moving boxes and crates around to make room for a shipment of goods. Talking was kept to a minimum, sounding more like the barking of orders from time to time than good-natured fun.

Alex glanced at the clock. One hour until the exchange.

Think, Alex. Think. You can do this.

She paused and wondered aloud. "What would Hawk do?"

Alex chuckled as she considered the answer to her own question.

"He'd probably give me some encouraging word that he first found in a fortune cookie somewhere and sell it as his own."

Seconds later, the lightning idea hit Alex. Her eyes widened and her pulse quickened. She needed to hurry if her plan was going to stand a chance.

CHAPTER 19

Khabas, Oman

FROM THE PASSENGER SEAT, Hawk looked up at the cloudless sky littered with stars. With the window rolled down, he felt comfortable amid the dissipating warmth. The northern coast of Oman had a well-documented reputation for unbearable heat, and Hawk appreciated the fact that his mission had been assigned under the cover of night.

"You almost forget how many stars there are when you live in the city," Hawk said, his eyes still scanning the heavens.

"They make you feel quite insignificant, don't they?" Ray said.

Hawk shrugged. "Any type of status we esteem to ourselves is nothing more than self-importance. If you never think more highly of yourself than you should, you never feel all that insignificant."

"You're quite the philosopher, Hawk."

"I fancy myself as one. But maybe it's because I've spent so much time hunkered down waiting out the enemy."

"That's not gonna happen tonight," Ray said. "You're going to go down there and meet him face to face."

The port came into view in the valley below before Ray pulled off to the side of the road.

"This is the end of the line for us," Ray said. "You're gonna take it from here."

Hawk turned and studied his friend's eyes. They drooped and sagged, maybe from a long day of driving—though Hawk wondered if Ray's weariness could be attributed to something else.

"You're still with me on this, right?" Hawk asked.

"Yeah, you bet," Ray said, his voice monotone.

"I mean it, Ray. I need to know that you're with me a hundred percent or else I'm just gonna take the money and run."

"Maybe that's what you should do anyway."

"Fifty grand is a nice haul, but I won't get far on that—and I'll struggle to work again."

"*Chuck Pearl* might struggle to work again, but you can just reinvent yourself. A new name, a new background, a new start. If I were you, I wouldn't think twice about it."

"Why do I get the feeling you're thinking twice about helping me? Is that what this is about?"

Ray pursed his lips and looked at the floorboard.

"It's not like that, Hawk. It's just that—"

"It's just that what? Now's not the time for subtle nuances. I need the cold hard truth. So dish it."

"I can't help you," Ray said. "I just can't do it. I have too much to lose if I go out on a limb like this."

Hawk sighed. "What happened to you, Ray? You were a patriot once and now—just look at yourself, slumming for this self-important jerk in Oman. You're a Navy Seal, not somebody's lackey. Make your break right now from him and let's take down Al Hasib and Karif Fazil in the most glorious way possible. Restore some honor to your name. Do what you're best at."

"Unfortunately, I am doing what I'm best at— maximizing my profits while minimizing my risk."

Hawk remained silent for a minute as he stared out the window.

"Don't make me do this alone," he said.

"You don't have to do it at all," Ray said. "That's what I'm trying to tell you. Just go. I'll handle it from here."

"No, I need to see this out. I need to take down Al Hasib once and for all. And if it means I don't make it out alive, then so be it. At least I went down swinging, which is more than I can say for your sorry ass right now."

"So now you're trying to shame me into helping you?"

"My call to arms didn't work," Hawk said. "I had to try a different tact. But I see you've dug your heels in here. That's your choice, but I'm disappointed. You told me yesterday that you'd help. But here you are going back on your word."

"I'm trying to help you here."

"What would help me is if you did what you said you were going to do."

Ray climbed out of the truck and walked around to the passenger side.

"She's all yours now, Hawk. Just go do whatever it is you're going to do. I'll be watching from here."

Hawk slid over into the driver's seat.

"And good luck, Hawk."

Hawk shook his head and jammed the truck into drive before stomping on the gas. With Ray unwilling to help, Hawk decided he would take his chances with a solo mission. He had placed several tracking devices on the weapons and in the containers in hopes that they would lead him straight to Fazil's latest hideout. Once Hawk had a chance to scope out the Al Hasib stronghold, he'd figure out a way to lure Fazil out into the open so he could capture him and deliver him to U.S. military forces, preferably with an audience. Conducting such a mission without Ray's help would be far more challenging, but Hawk concluded his other choices would mean four more years of Michaels, four more years of living on the lam, and four more years of not seeing Alex. To Hawk, that wasn't an alternative he could live with.

The truck rumbled down a steep incline toward the harbor, which was surprisingly well lit. Hawk considered for a moment that conducting an illegal weapons exchange in plain sight was dangerous, but in Khabas, Oman, who would really care that much? Every potential law enforcement officer or military personnel was likely paid off already and well versed in the art of turning a blind eye.

Hawk came to a stop and turned right, following the signs for the seaport. He didn't get more than a half-mile farther down the road before he noticed a roadblock up ahead. Ray had left him proper documentation, but the closer Hawk got, the more his uneasiness grew about the situation.

What is a roadblock doing here at this time of night?

That's when Hawk recognized the military vehicle in the roadblock as one belonging to the U.S. military.

Damn it. I'm being set up.

In an instant, everything became clear to Hawk. What he'd identified as reluctance on the part of Ray was actually guilt. Ray was trying to deal with his betrayal of a former colleague. Despite their differences, a strong bond still existed—and Hawk realized Ray was struggling with his decision.

Hawk slammed on the brakes and threw the truck into reverse. He wasn't sure what he was going to do, but he wasn't about to drive straight into military custody. Before he could complete a three-point turn and change his direction, the truck being used for the road accelerated after him.

Stomping on the gas pedal, Hawk gripped the steering wheel, his hands starting to hurt from the pressure he exerted on it. His eyes bounced between the desolate road ahead and his rearview mirror. The truck was gaining on him and he had no real options.

In a moment of desperation, Hawk maneuvered his truck off the road and across the desert sand. The truck tailing him did likewise. Both vehicles bounced along for about a mile before a rockier terrain prevented Hawk from going any farther. He tried to back out of the pocket he'd driven into, but the trailing truck roared up from behind and trapped him.

Several moments later, a pair of Humvees joined them in a strong show of force. Hawk threw his head back and screamed in frustration.

A pair of armed soldiers approached Hawk, keeping their guns trained on him. Hawk raised his hands in surrender.

"I'm unarmed," Hawk said as one of the soldiers

opened the door.

A guard snatched Hawk by his shirt and dragged him out of the truck.

"Take it easy, man," Hawk said. "I'm going peaceably here."

"The irony," the Army Ranger said. "The man selling weapons to one of the most deadly terrorist forces on the planet is *going peaceably*."

"What is this all about?" Hawk asked.

"Perhaps you're the one who should be answering that question yourself. We're not the ones trying to sell weapons to Al Hasib."

"What are you talking about? You have no proof of that."

The soldier chuckled and shook his head. "We actually have a truckload of proof. Now, hands behind your head."

Hawk complied with the order before a pair of handcuffs was ratcheted down on his wrists.

"The great Brady Hawk finally arrested," one of the soldiers said. "I didn't think it'd be so easy or that he'd look so harmless."

"All those stories must be embellished."

Hawk glared at them. "I can assure you that they're not."

"Great. You can tell them to me all over again during our transport back to the U.S. The president wants to talk with you personally before you're turned over to the judicial system."

"President Michaels?" Hawk asked.

The soldier nodded. "The one and only."

"President Michaels wants to see me?"

"I didn't stutter."

"Don't you find that odd?" Hawk asked.

"Not any more odd than a former Navy Seal trying to peddle weapons to Al Hasib in Oman during the middle of the night."

The guard shoved Hawk in the back, forcing him toward one of the Humvees.

When Hawk stepped inside, his mouth went slack-jawed at the sight of Ray.

"I tried to warn you," Ray said.

Hawk narrowed his eyes. "How could you do this to me?"

"Just following orders."

"Whose orders?"

"The president of the United States. Now, I'll be right back. I have to go deliver some weapons as promised to some terrorist friends of mine."

Hawk watched as Ray climbed out of the vehicle and jumped behind the wheel of the weapons truck. As he drove away, he gave a mocking salute to Hawk.

"Where's he going?" Hawk asked.

"He's going to finish the mission," a soldier said.

CHAPTER 20

Washington, D.C.

MICHAELS STUDIED SEVERAL PAPERS written by his aides as he wound down his day. The latest poll had him ahead of Braxton by 10 percentage points. Once the electoral college projections were factored, Michaels' lead swelled to a commanding 130 votes more than his opponent. Most political pundits were on the verge of suggesting that the presidential race was already over. By virtue of Michaels' big lead, he could focus on policies rather than partisan politics.

A knock on the door interrupted him as he looked up to see David Kriegel poking his head inside.

"Catching up on the latest poll numbers?" Kriegel asked.

Michaels shook his head. "I've got more important issues to attend to, like shaping the direction of the nation for the next four years."

"So you have seen the most recent reports, haven't you?" Kriegel said as he strode over to the chair in front of Michaels' desk.

Michaels smiled wryly and set his papers down. "I may have taken a peek at them earlier today."

"Well then, are you ready for some more good news?"

"I've always got time for that."

"Just heard back about your mystery accuser. Turns out she's quite prolific when it comes to getting arrested. Her rap sheet is several paper reams long with her latest arrest for driving under the influence with cocaine in her system. She's being cued up to be featured prominently on the news next week if she continues these allegations."

"What you're saying is that everyone will dismiss her as a nutcase?"

"There will always be a handful of people who would believe some story like that, but I'm pretty sure this one won't see the light of day."

"Good work. Anything else?"

"I saved the best for last."

Michaels leaned forward, his hands clasped together and resting on his desk.

"Don't keep me in suspense any longer."

"I just received a call from the Pentagon. The

Army Rangers captured Brady Hawk in Oman attempting to sell weapons to Al Hasib."

Michaels shook his head. "Hawk has some nerve, doesn't he?"

"My favorite part is that they weren't even weapons from Colton Industries."

"Let's get that going in the cable news cycle, shall we? More stories like this should bolster my poll rankings. I may not even have to stump that much the way things are going."

Kriegel held up his finger. "Let's wait on this Hawk capture for a couple of days. We'll get much better optics on this story on Monday after your debate with Braxton, which is supposed to center around national security. But Tuesday morning, we'll hit this hard."

"Excellent idea," Michaels said as he pumped his fist. "I love it. I'll hammer away at Braxton Monday and then Tuesday we serve up results."

"I'm glad you approve. I'll get everything together, including some official U.S. Army video to go along with the story when we release it."

"How the mighty have fallen," Michaels said.

Kriegel excused himself, leaving Michaels alone with his papers. He could sense victory finally arriving and the man who'd been one of the biggest banes of his political career would go away forever.

And J.D. Blunt, you're next.

CHAPTER 21

Brighton, England

ALEX WATCHED EVERY moment of the capture unfold on her monitor. Her face flushed red with rage as she watched the Army Rangers swarm around Hawk's vehicle and stick him in one of their Humvees. Meanwhile, she continued to type furiously on her laptop. After a few more minutes, she took a break to call Blunt. She needed to vent with the only person who would understand.

"I tried," she said after he picked up the phone.

"What happened?" Blunt asked.

"I tried to warn him but he left before I could respond back to him, and he walked right into the trap Michaels laid for him," she said as she fought back tears.

Alex wanted to scream or curl up in a ball and cry until there were no more tears left—both options sounded appealing to her in the moment. But there wasn't time for that.

"Try to keep it together, Alex. We'll figure a way out of this."

"What do you think is going to happen? Is Michaels going to suddenly have a change of heart and let Hawk walk free?"

"Hawk did the same to Michaels. Maybe he'll return the favor?"

"Are you even hearing yourself, J.D.? Michaels is a mad man with no intention of doing anything favorable for Hawk, especially now that the cat is out of the bag regarding Michaels' true intentions. Make no mistake, Michaels is going to do whatever he can to silence Hawk."

"Sadly, I know you're right, but that doesn't mean something couldn't change. Perhaps Michaels will require services in the future. Not even Michaels is a big enough fool to pass up utilizing Hawk in that manner."

Alex clenched her fists as she stood up and paced around the room.

"Hawk would rather die than join forces with Michaels. You ought to know that as well as anyone. Hawk is loyal to a fault. I don't need to tell you that's how he got into this mess in the first place, trusting one of his cronies from the Seals."

"Michaels has a strange way of exerting pressure in just the right places to get what he wants."

"But Hawk would never do anything for Michaels, no matter what. We've got to do something or else it's lights out."

"Perhaps you're right," Blunt said. "But what can we do from our positions at the moment? I have friends in high places, but I doubt any of them would risk their careers to help in this situation. Michaels is just too powerful."

"There is something *I* can do."

"Care to share that with me?"

"You'll know it when you see it."

"Alex, what are you planning on doing? Please tell me you're not preparing to go after him."

"I'm desperate, but I'm not insane."

"Alex," Blunt said, speaking in a measured tone. "What are you going to do?"

She sat back down at her laptop and continued typing.

"Alex, talk to me. Tell me what you're doing."

She smiled. "It's not what I'm going to do, but what I've already done."

"Since you're sitting in your apartment in England, I'm starting to get concerned."

"Relax, J.D. I just stole an MQ-9 Reaper—and I need to divert my full attention to flying it."

Alex hung up and zeroed in on her keyboard as she entered new coordinates for the drone she'd hacked. The nearest one she found was only fifty miles away from Hawk's location, which meant she could have the Reaper onsite in less than 15 minutes.

She took a deep breath and exhaled slowly as she pulled up the drone's camera and put it up on one of her other monitors. Her laptop became the virtual on-board computer, enabling her to identify targets as they came into view. With the DOD satellite picture still up on another screen, she marked the vehicle Hawk was in. They'd only been traveling less than five minutes, but it was far enough to get clear of the pop-ulated portion of the city. While the Humvee sped along an empty highway, Alex plotted her next move.

Getting Hawk out of custody was her top prior-ity, but she didn't want to kill any Rangers in the process. The last thing she wanted was to move to the top of a terrorist watch list. To get a better idea of how she should attack with the drone, she circled the small convoy of three armored Humvees. The dis-tance between the trucks was tight but ideal for mak-ing a quick strike and diverting the drone elsewhere.

She directed the drone to make one more final pass before she settled on the best tactic to accomplish all her goals. Engaging the Reaper's missile system, she set a target for fifty feet in front of the lead vehicle.

Hawk was in the middle Humvee and would likely smash into the back of the front one. All she could do was hope and pray that nothing worse happened and that Hawk could find a way to get free.

Here goes nothing.

Alex keyed in the command to launch the missile. She held her breath as it rocketed toward its target.

CHAPTER 22

Khabas, Oman

HAWK SAT SILENTLY in the back of the Humvee as it bounced along the pothole infested stretch of Omani highway. He studied the two Rangers who sat opposite from him in the modified vehicle. Mostly still dressed in their tactical gear, they removed their helmets and lit up celebratory cigarettes. Hawk coughed and one of the soldiers cracked the window. And most importantly to Hawk, they seemed confident that their prisoner was secure. With his feet shackled to the floorboard and his hands bound in cuffs, Hawk didn't appear to be going anywhere.

"This road is going to rattle my teeth out," the soldier who went by the name of Nettles said.

"Reminds me of driving in Chicago," replied his colleague named Zisk.

"You ever drive in Chicago, Hawk?" Nettles asked.

Hawk shook his head.

"You aren't very talkative," Zisk said. "Guess that's to be expected when you're a Navy wuss and you get captured by a bunch of Army Rangers."

"It wasn't exactly a fair fight," Hawk said.

Nettles threw his hands in the air. "Oh, he speaks."

"But he's whining," Zisk said, before transitioning into a mocking voice. "He's crying to mommy because it wasn't fair. I thought Navy Seals were the greatest soldiers on earth."

Nettles chuckled. "Look, we get it. Guys who go to the Seals are soldiers who know they'd never make it as a Ranger. But don't think you're gonna get any sympathy from us. You're a traitor to your own country. You don't deserve a fair fight."

Hawk bit his lip and shook his head. He couldn't blame the pair of soldiers for feeling the way they did. If the shoe were on the other foot, Hawk knew he'd feel the same sort of disdain for them as they felt for him. But the sniping wasn't easy to listen to.

"He's gone back to being silent Hawk," Nettles said.

"Do you think he talks with the terrorists or simply mimes for them?" Zisk asked before laughing at his own comment.

"You two should get your own comedy show," Hawk quipped.

"Well, the joke's on you tonight," Nettles said. "We just took down one of the most wanted terrorists in U.S. history."

Sufficiently annoyed, Hawk decided to confront their ignorance head on. "Is that how they referred to me in your bullshit briefing? A most wanted terrorist?"

"Don't flatter yourself," Zisk said. "Your buddy Karif Fazil is still number one."

"Yet you picked him over me?" Hawk said. "Guess we know who the real losers are now. Yep, comedy suits you two better."

"What are you talking about?" Zisk said. "You weren't selling to Fazil tonight. That was some Pakistani low life."

Nettles shook his head and blew a plume of smoke toward the cracked window. "Yeah, don't try to play us as fools. The truth is you were just trying to make some quick cash off some weapons you got from daddy Colton."

"So, that was the official narrative?" Hawk asked. "Not bad. Not bad at all. But it was a complete lie. If you don't believe me, go be real heroes. Turn this Humvee around and go obliterate a bunch of Al Hasib operatives."

Nettles and Zisk both took long drags on their cigarettes and glared at Hawk.

"You expect us to believe that?" Zisk asked. "Boy, you Navy punks really are stupider than you look."

Nettles started to say something before a faint humming sound from outside the vehicle arrested their attention.

"Is that what I think it is?" Zisk asked.

"Sure as hell sounds like a Reaper to me," Nettles said.

"I don't remember anything from the briefing about drone support for this mission, do you?" Zisk asked.

"No. Nothing. That sure is odd."

But after a few seconds, everything clicked for Hawk.

Alex!

Hawk heard the plane circle their position once more. He shifted in his seat as far against the door as he could and braced for impact.

By his best calculation, the amount of time it took for the missile to rocket off the drone and strike the highway was less than two seconds. The last thing he saw before the explosion was wide-eyed looks on the faces of Nettles and Zisk.

The lead Humvee didn't have time to stop for the large crater created by the missile when it struck the road. A nosedive into the flaming hole led to the vehicle catching fire before the soldiers inside scrambled out to safety.

The Humvee trailing Hawk had enough time to slow down before crashing into the bumper. The Rangers exited and raced to check on the other soldiers in the first vehicle.

But Hawk's Humvee had its own story. The blast happened so fast that the driver didn't have time to stop, sending the vehicle careening into the leader. Inside, Nettles and Zisk flew forward and hit their heads on the plate glass separating the front and back seats. Zisk crumpled to the floor but Nettles' body came to rest on the bench next to Hawk.

Hawk scooted close to Nettles and rooted around in his pockets for the keys. Upon locating them, Hawk worked quickly to release his feet first and then his hands. He snatched Zisk's weapon and grabbed a flash bomb, which he dropped on the road next to their vehicle. Hawk covered his head in a fetal position and waited for the device to detonate.

Once the explosion rocked the road, Hawk burst out of the vehicle and sprinted toward the trailing Humvee. He climbed inside and took off. Several bullets hit the back of the armor-plated vehicle and fell harmlessly to the side.

Hawk jammed his foot on the accelerator and stared at the road ahead of him, taking glances in the rearview mirror at the fireball engulfing the middle of the highway.

Nice work, Alex.

But Hawk still had plenty to do if he was going mitigate the disaster that Michaels had created due to his giant ego. Hawk could already imagine the video feed of him being frog marched into court and the national media smearing his good name. Tom Colton and Colton Industries would be brought into the story as well, leading to a revival of narratives about American weapons exports and how it was ruining the world. Eventually, Blunt and Alex would get dragged into the fray as well, embarrassing their families and sullying their character by one Michaels administration lie spoon fed to the media after another.

Hawk determined not to let any of that happen. He didn't want Michaels getting an ounce of credit for taking out Al Hasib or its leader, not for personal reasons but out of principle.

Any man who tries to arm the enemy for political gain doesn't deserve the slightest bit of praise.

However, Hawk knew if he didn't catch Ray in the truck before he reached the port, stopping such treasonous activity would be far more challenging if not lethal. He narrowed his eyes as he bore down on the first vehicle he'd encountered since leaving the scene of his getaway. As Hawk drew nearer, he recognized the same truck he'd been confined to for hours. And while Ray drove with purpose, Hawk could tell the former Navy Seal wasn't anticipating any hostiles on the road.

Pulling alongside Ray from the left-hand lane, Hawk rammed his Humvee into the side of the truck. Ray's vehicle swerved off the road but maintained its speed. Hawk glanced to his right to see Ray glaring back before jerking his wheel to the left and bumping Hawk. However, the Humvee held stout. Hawk whipped back into the truck and bounced back. He repeated this maneuver three more times before the last hit sent Ray out of control.

Ray's truck hit a rock and bounced high in the air, fishtailing for about a thirty meters before spinning out into the desert. Undaunted, Ray turned the truck around and headed back toward the highway. Hawk, who'd stopped to watch for a moment to see what Ray would do, restarted the collision protocol. Ray weakly tapped Hawk first before he retaliated by laying hard into the side of Ray's truck. On the second series of exchanges, Hawk only needed two hits before he knocked Ray off the road—only this time Ray didn't come back.

Teetering from side to side, Ray's vehicle lost its center mass and toppled to the ground, skidding along on the passenger's side for about fifty meters. Hawk decided against watching from afar and roared up next to the crippled truck.

The driver's side door flung open, revealing an armed Ray. Clutching a pistol in his right hand, he climbed out and staggered to the ground. A gash on his forehead resulted in a fresh stream of blood that marred his face. His shoulder also drooped as he winced every time he reached over and touched it.

Meanwhile, Hawk was already braced against the hood of the Humvee, his rifle trained on Ray.

"This is the end of the line, Ray," Hawk said.

"What are you gonna do, Hawk? You gonna shoot me? Killing me won't solve anything. Michaels will just trot out some other lackey to accomplish his agenda."

Hawk shrugged. "I'm not trying to stop everything that lame excuse for a leader is going to do. But I am going to make sure nothing happens tonight."

Ray chuckled. "And this from a man who suggested just giving working weapons to Al Hasib."

Hawk shook his head. "Wanna open up the back here and make a little bet?"

Ray didn't flinch.

"I bet you that there isn't a single sabotaged weapon in that entire shipment there," Hawk said. "You know I'm right, don't you?"

Ray remained quiet.

"I figured it all out, Ray. It all dawned on me, this whole ruse you and Ackerman were running."

"This wasn't the original plan," Ray said. "But Ackerman knew that Michaels was after you."

"And how did he know who I was? Did you tell him, Ray?"

"The moment you showed your face, I let him know what was up."

"So, I did that whole Chuck Pearl routine just for his own amusement?"

"Pretty much," Ray said. "He's got a twisted sense of humor."

"So do you. You were the one who made a mockery of me, blew my cover, delivered me to the clueless Rangers. This was all one very big elaborate setup."

"We were just gonna deliver the weapons. No one would've been the wiser."

Hawk nodded. "You're right. No one would've been. But you and Ackerman are opportunists, aren't you? Just like Michaels."

"I'm not going to apologize for anything. Never look a gift horse in the mouth, right? Plus, I still hold you accountable for what happened that night in Jalabad. You checked out on us—and it nearly got us all killed."

"We all deserved to die that night for what we did."

"Everything isn't always neat and tidy as you

want it to be. Sometimes, the only way you can get what you want is to step over the line."

Hawk kicked at the sand. "That's not the kind of man I am—at least not anymore."

"No, you're the great Brady Hawk, so great that his own country views him as a homegrown terrorist."

"That's a questionable perspective, one I take serious issue with."

"I don't know what your end game is, but you don't really have much of a play now."

Hawk raised his weapon. "Drop your gun, Ray. I'm done talking."

"No you're not because I'm not going to drop anything."

Hawk fired off a short burst that peppered the ground near Ray's feet.

"Put the gun down now," Hawk bellowed.

Ray crouched down and lowered his gun, setting it in the dirt.

"They're watching you, Hawk," Ray said. "Several of my guys are up on that ridge and they've got you in their sights. I would advise you to put your weapon down before someone puts a bullet in your head."

Hawk looked up at the ridge, which was more than a mile away.

"I'd love to see one of your guards attempt that

shot. No one that good is working private security in Oman."

"Pride comes before a fall."

"And bullshit comes before truth whenever you're talking. Now, step clear of the vehicle and get face down in the dirt, hands behind your head."

Ray complied. "You're making a big mistake."

"The mistake I made was coming to you for help and thinking you'd changed," Hawk said. "But you're the same asshole you were when we were Seals together. You just make more money now."

"Michaels is gonna find you and kill you, Hawk. If not tonight, some other time. He's not gonna let you get away with thwarting his plans."

"We'll see about that."

Hawk kept his rifle trained on Ray as he walked over to the toppled truck. He opened the back and several crates spilled out onto the ground. Snatching up one of the handheld RPGs, Hawk backed up and took aim at the vehicle.

"This is me thwarting Michaels' plan," Hawk said before squeezing the trigger and lighting up the truck. An explosion blew out the side of the truck facing upward. In a split second, fire engulfed the weapons and started consuming the truck.

Hawk glanced back down at Ray, who was reaching for a gun in his ankle holster.

"I don't think so," Hawk said, glancing down at his captive.

"I'm gonna make you shoot me," Ray said before he reached for the weapon.

Hawk hit Ray in the leg. "Satisfied now?"

Ray screamed in agony. "That was my knee cap, you asshole."

"You can thank me some other time when I see you."

Ray growled and lunged for his gun again. However, Hawk realized Ray had no inclination to stop.

Two bullets—one to the chest, the other to the head.

Ray's body went limp.

"It didn't have to end that way, Ray."

Hawk climbed into the Humvee and headed for the ridge. When he arrived there a few minutes later, the Fortress Security personnel were set up and waiting. Lying in prone positions, they had their rifles sighted in on Hawk and unleashed a furious attack. Bullets whizzed past Hawk, some dinging off the side of his truck's armor. The relentless assault continued as he pressed forward, even after he parked his Humvee a few meters away from them.

Hawk stuck his head through the cutout in the roof so he could operate the gun turret. After offering the men a chance to surrender, Hawk took aim at the men. He unleashed several rounds of ammunition on the guards, shooting every one of them.

He shot the tires out of the truck just in case any of them somehow managed to survive. With that portion of his mission complete, he slid back down into the driver's seat, just in time to see a huge explosion send flames lapping the dark knight sky.

Alex—that woman never stops.

As Hawk contemplated his next move, the Reaper returned and circled around the ridge twice before striking off in a different direction. But Hawk understood what Alex was trying to tell him. She wanted him to follow the drone. And that's what he did.

Hawk tailed the drone from the ground for 20 minutes before happening upon an airstrip. A C-130 sat at one end of the runway where the bay door was guarded by a pair of military policemen. Hawk roared up to the door and got out, training his rifle on the men. They appeared caught off guard by Hawk's brash entry.

"Gentlemen, I'm going to need a ride," Hawk said.

The guards looked at each other, mouths agape.

CHAPTER 23

Washington, D.C.

VICE PRESIDENT NOAH YOUNG wondered how he failed to remain president after filling in for Michaels when he was in the public's crosshairs. Everything seemed primed for Young to sneak into the Oval Office through the figurative backdoor. But Michaels managed to turn what should've been a prompt exit into his own version of the Phoenix.

Young concluded that Americans are always suckers for a comeback story, especially one where the hero rises from the ashes. For most of his tenure, Michaels had been reviled by the American people and his own party. Nothing he did seemed to placate anyone, even while a collective list of grievances held by average citizens compounded daily with each political misstep. Eventually, Michaels had sunk so far to the bottom that his pathway to the top started with digging himself out of the mud. And he was mired in it.

Despite Michaels' impossible situation, Young marveled at how the president had managed to rewrite history while also using his past to endear him to the American people. Without a doubt, Michaels' revival during his first term was one of the most unlikely in the modern era. But Young knew the real story.

The real credit needed to be bestowed upon the Washington spin doctors, the masters of the Beltway. Instead of letting Michaels languish in his past sins, these manipulators of the public's collective consciousness rebuilt the president's image through a series of targeted campaigns to present a soft and gentler side of Michaels. Instead of a no-nonsense leader, a smattering of White House videos, staged photo ops, and footage from allegedly random cell phones that captured the president being human all found their way into social media streams that eventually trended on various websites and apps. Michaels had not only returned, but he'd returned in better shape than he'd ever been in.

And Young loathed every moment of it. The American people had been duped into believing Michaels was actually a decent human being. Young knew the truth.

Young's phone rang from an unknown number.

"Hello?"

"Noah, this is J.D. Blunt. Can you talk right now?"

"Sure. What do you want?"

"To be honest, I want my life back—and I want Michaels gone."

"Good luck with that," Young said. "That ship sailed a long time ago. We have the most forgiving populace on the planet."

"They might be forgiving, but they certainly don't like being made fools of."

"And who's making fools of them?"

"Your boss is. He's continuing to play this game in the shadows and has gotten away with it so far. But you can put a stop to that."

"How exactly do you expect me to do that? Anything I do now could be considered a power grab, especially right before the election. I'd even be sabotaging my own political career."

"Did you take this job because you wanted to further your political career? Or did you take it because you wanted to help your country?"

Young sighed. "I did it because I thought I could actually make a difference, but now . . ."

"You still can make a difference if you help get Michaels out of office and save America from his meddling ways. Leaving him in a position of power will result in some dark days ahead. He's in danger of destabilizing the entire Middle East even more so than it already is and empowering terrorists to bring their tactics to U.S. soil."

"You know how I feel about him."

"I do, which is why I'm coming to you with this plea to help stop him."

"So, what exactly can I do? I can't forcibly remove him."

"Everything will take care of itself if you do what I tell you," Blunt said. "You can assure that his reputation is destroyed once and for all. All the questions that will arise should result in some heated congressional hearings. And I don't even think his party will want to defend him after the truth surfaces."

"What do you think he's going to confess to? He's still never admitted he ever did anything wrong."

"If he thinks he's talking to you as his trusted vice president, he might let his guard down."

"That's a big *if*. I certainly am not under any illusion that he trusts me."

"But he might," Blunt said. "Give him a reason to. You can come up with something."

"And then you just expect him to magically divulge the darkest of secrets that will end his aspirations at another term and could possibly land him in prison?"

"I know it might be a long shot, but it's one of the few we have at this point. If there was another way. . ."

Young huffed a short breath through his nose. "There's always another way."

"Not necessarily legal ones. This one needs to happen the right way. We're not a banana republic—at least, not yet anyway."

"Do you have proof of what he's doing?"

"Wikileaks has already shown what he's up to."

"But only the tinfoil hat wearers believe that, which is a small part of the population. The media has moved on from that story. It's been relegated to the trash heap that is fake news."

"All you need to do is have him tell you what he's done. Once that recording goes public, the media won't be able to ignore that story."

"I'll give it a shot," Young said. "But I wouldn't get my hopes up. If there's anything I've learned about Michaels while working with him over the past four years, it's that he is savvy and can see things coming far before anyone else."

"That's all I can ask for."

"Just don't call me again," Young said. "I don't want to raise any suspicion. I'll call you from another number."

Blunt gave Young his number before they ended their call.

Young immediately dialed Michaels' secretary. She was always helpful with his requests and found a 15-minute window she could squeeze him into later that afternoon.

* * *

YOUNG ENTERED MICHAELS' OFFICE and strode across the room before taking a seat across from the president. Michaels' head was buried in a document and he didn't bother to look up.

"What is it, Noah?" he asked. "I don't know if you can tell, but I'm extremely busy these days."

"I understand, but I wanted to talk about something I heard."

Michaels sighed and dropped the papers on his desk. "Oh, great. Now the rumor mill is creating interruptions in my day. What is it this time?"

"Don't act like this is some intrusion into your work time. What I'm about to ask you about might be what saves your presidency."

"As if that's something you care about, seeing how as recently as a year ago you tried to steal my chair."

Young shook his head. "I was just following the protocol of the United States Constitution. When you're relieved of duty, I take over. It's really very simple. And do I need to remind you that you willingly stepped down during the investigation?"

"Will you get on with it? Unlike you, I'm not just a figurehead."

"As you wish," Young said. "I wanted to speak with you today because I heard that it's possible that you may have been sending arms to some—how shall I say it—non-state actors in the Middle East?"

"This is a rumor now? Wikileaks splashed this all over their front page a few days ago—but the story was deemed contrived. Besides, I'd never send weapons to any terrorists. I'm insulted that you'd believe such an accusation for even a split second, especially after it has been debunked."

"I'm not talking about Wikileaks," Young said. "I've heard this from several other sources. Apparently, there's more to this than just a recording."

"A manipulated recording," Michaels said, wagging his finger. "And I don't know who your sources are, but they're lying to you."

"Look, maybe you're trying to protect me with plausible deniability and all that, but I need to know if you're arming terrorists. I don't want to get blindsided by anything."

"For the last time, no. I'm not privy to any such action, no matter how sure your sources are that this is happening. It simply isn't true."

"Okay," Young said as he stood up. "Thank you for your candor. I'll leave you alone to finish your work."

Michaels looked back down at his papers and waved with the back of his hand dismissively at Young.

"Don't bother me again with this type of garbage. It's not worth my time to respond."

Young exited quickly and returned to his office. He wasted no time in calling Blunt.

"How'd it go?" Blunt asked.

"You're gonna have to find another way," Young said. "Michaels didn't go for the bait."

"Not even a nibble?"

"Nothing. Even with me, he's holding fast to the line that it's all contrived, a witch hunt by his detractors."

"That bastard."

"He didn't rise to that office without some serious political savvy."

"Well, I'm not sure I've got any bullets left in my gun," Blunt said. "Michaels' ability to duck and dodge every scandal is bewildering. Short of shooting him in the head, I'm not sure there is a way to remove him from his position."

"What about Hawk?"

"You want Hawk to assassinate Michaels?"

"I'm not suggesting any such thing. Your words, not mine."

Blunt grunted. "I want this done through some type of legal channels. We're not going to stoop to

Michaels' level. Besides, even if I did suggest that to Hawk, he wouldn't do it. He's too much of a patriot, even if the end justifies the means."

"No, no. I mean, perhaps there's another way Hawk could pressure Michaels, maybe even get him to admit what he's done."

"That'd take some serious logistics and insider help. And I'm afraid we don't have that many allies at the moment. Everyone sees where this election is going and they want to saddle their horse to the winning cart. I'd be lucky to get any favors at this point."

"Fine," Young said. "I just wanted to let you know that I did what I could."

"Well, hang tight. There might another way—a legal way. I'll call you soon."

Young hung up and spun around in his chair. He stared out the office window, wondering if the view might be his for the next four years—or only the next four weeks. The way he saw the situation unfolding, Michaels was in an all-or-nothing scenario. Prison or four more years—a strange pairing of options, but there was no other alternative as far as Young could see.

As much as he enjoyed his position and all the accoutrements that went along with it, Young had long since concluded he could part with everything—if it meant the removal of Michaels as president.

CHAPTER 24

HAWK HAD LAID LOW for two days at Hohenfels with General Van Fortner before attempting to re-enter the U.S. Despite toting a plethora of passports crafted for the various legends Hawk held, traveling commercially was a risky proposition. He needed something sure, something solid. Fortner stepped in again to help.

After a conversation with Blunt, Fortner informed Hawk that his best chance to get to Washington would be on a C-17 military transport plane. Assigning Hawk to the next flight leaving Hohenfels for Washington, Fortner expressed how he'd done all he could do and wished Hawk good luck.

Once the C-17 landed on U.S. soil, Hawk rented a room for a couple of weeks at an extended stay hotel. He rented a car and promptly changed the plates, swapping them with another rental vehicle he identified in the hotel parking lot across the street from his. Once Hawk was confident that he'd eliminated any chance of getting happened upon by local law enforcement, he started to piece together his plan. He'd read that Michaels was planning on heading to Camp David the next day. That was all Hawk needed to begin planning his next move.

Hawk called Alex, who followed their protocol for voice contact in the event of an emergency. While technically far away from a crisis situation, Hawk needed to connect with Alex, if anything for his own sanity. He wanted her stamp of approval for his proposed plan of attack as well as enlisting her help for live support.

"So, what do you think?" Hawk asked. "What pitfalls am I overlooking?"

She remained silent for nearly half a minute, causing Hawk to wonder if they'd become disconnected or perhaps something worse—Michaels' minions had managed to track her down to Brighton.

But her smooth voice eliminated his concern, which turned out to be unfounded.

"I'm worried that this won't work," she said. "There are too many opportunities for this thing to go sideways. And the minute it does, you're gone—and gone forever."

"Living out my days in Terre Haute wouldn't be the worst thing that could happen to me," Hawk said.

"That federal prison won't take too kindly to you. Michaels will gleefully send you there, where you'll be assaulted daily by Al Hasib operatives who have been captured and convicted to life sentences."

"We're obviously talking in hypotheticals here—and such outcomes are unlikely. Besides, we both know this is going to work."

"I'd rather you wait, Hawk. I have my own plan already set in motion, one that you may not even have to lift a finger to see through."

She explained the details of how she intended to imperil Michaels' re-election campaign and asked Hawk for his feedback.

"Depending on others to do the dirty work is never a great tactic," Hawk said. "The moment someone goes off script, you're in trouble. And you'll never be able to get things back. Winding up the clock and turning it loose? Not a surefire approach."

"Well, it's too late," she said. "The plan has already been set in motion."

"What if this gets in my way?"

"Then I'll send you in to make sure everything runs smoothly. See? Problem solved."

Hawk chuckled. "I'm glad to see that over the past nine months you're still as sassy as ever."

"And you haven't lost any of your bravado. But seriously, I'd rather you wait and see before you storm the castle. I really think my plan is going to work, and the less we stay out of the crosshairs, the better as it pertains to our future."

"If we wait on this, it may not matter. Once Michaels is re-elected, all bets are off."

"This won't take that long."

"But you want to rely on the legal system to handle this. When was the last time they ever delivered for you?"

"Stop being so stubborn, Hawk. Think of this as the kind of operation that requires weeks, not hours. It's going to work."

"Let's suppose for a moment that your plan is flawless. You've accounted for everything, including the variables of how certain people might react when placed in a pressure cooker of a situation like you've created. Even if you're right, how long will this take before Michaels is gone and behind bars? Months? Years? We simply don't have that long, not for our own sake or for the sake of the country. If Michaels remains in power, God only knows the destruction that we'll suffer at the hands of this maniac. We're liable to have another 9-11 all over again, only this time it could be far worse."

"But charging in and handling it like a vigilante

amounts to nothing more than anarchy—and that's not good for the country in the long run either. You'll open up Pandora's box with that and will never be able to put it back."

Hawk sighed. "I'm going to be vigilant, but not a vigilante. I'll make him do the right thing."

"If you're making him do anything, he'll fight back. He needs to *choose* to resign."

"What makes you think Michaels would ever be humble enough to walk away without a fight?"

"I expect a fight, but he's going to lose. The American people are going to find out exactly what kind of monster he is. But don't worry—I have a fail-safe."

"You're counting on me to handle this if it doesn't work out?"

Alex chuckled. "When I was planning things, I wasn't sure I could count on you getting out alive. So, I went with my next best option."

"And who's that?"

"Just don't go right now, Hawk. Promise me that you'll wait for a few days and let me keep you updated on what's happening."

"I don't know, Alex. Sitting by idly isn't my style."

"Just promise me, Hawk. Okay? That's what I need to hear right now."

"I promise to proceed with caution."

"Hawk!"

"It's the best I can do, Alex. I'm not gonna lie to you."

"Fine. I'll take what I can get. But use extreme caution. Understand?"

"I'll do my best."

Hawk hung up and stared out the window at the Washington cityscape sprawling below. He vowed to honor his word to Alex, but he knew he wouldn't sit around and wait long.

Something's got to give—and it's not going to be me.

CHAPTER 25

Camp David, Maryland

PRESIDENT MICHAELS APPROACHED the tee box with a swagger that didn't quite fit his golf game. Since taking office nearly four years prior, he'd discovered that his skill level had increased significantly. He attributed his improvement to the fact that he had more access to more courses than he'd ever had before—and he took full advantage of them.

He leaned down and put a ball on top of a tee and slid it into the ground. Once he straightened upright, he glanced back over his shoulder to see David Kriegel whispering something to another aide. Kriegel covered his mouth with his hand, but Michaels knew what he was saying. Undoubtedly, Kriegel had launched into a diatribe about the terrible optics of golfing so close to the election. He'd implored Michaels to forego the outing and attend a nearby rally.

But Michaels refused to listen.

"The people want to know that I'm normal," Michaels said as he argued with Kriegel. "Playing golf is a way for me to show them that I'm just like them."

"But your average voter doesn't play golf. They all see it as a rich man's game," Kriegel fired back.

"It hardly costs anything to play a round. What are you talking about?"

Kriegel shook his head and didn't say a word.

Michaels believed he knew better than Kriegel, who Michaels believed rarely offered any sound advice. Kriegel was there to be a sounding board, not to sound off. But when he dared to speak his mind, Michaels plugged both ears.

Michaels gave Kriegel one more glance before addressing the ball. Recoiling slowly, Michaels unleashed a vicious swing that sent the ball hurtling forward—and to the left.

"Damn it," Michaels muttered as he watched his shot hook toward a patch of trees.

Michaels handed his club to his caddy and lumbered forward. The three senators he was playing with had all hit their balls straight and left them squarely in the middle of the fairway. And while Michaels had the honor of hitting last as the winner of the previous hole, such a position gave him no advantage. He squandered it when his shot landed deep in the wooded boundary.

"You'll be all right, Mr. President," one of the senators said as he continued forward.

"You're not kidding I'll be all right," Michaels said under his breath. "You know I'm going to come back and win this hole."

At least, that's how it almost always went. Michaels' tee shot would veer off course, but he'd make up for it with his short iron game.

Michaels snatched a 3-iron from his bag and told his caddy to wait along the fairway. The search for the lost ball lasted all of two minutes. Unable to locate the ball, Michaels fished one out of his pocket and dropped it on the ground, kicking it to a favorable lie before announcing that he'd found his shot.

He took a deep breath and gauged the best route out of the woods before he stepped up to the ball. Then he froze when he felt a cold metal object shoved into his back.

"Don't move," a man said.

Michaels froze.

"That's right. Stay right there," the man said.

"You're never going to get away with this," Michaels said. "You do realize there's a Secret Service detail following me everywhere."

"But they can't see you here, you cheating bastard, because you decided to toss a ball onto the ground," the man said as he held a ball out in front of Michaels. "Here's your ball, you piece of shit."

Michaels turned around slowly and came face to face with Oliver Ackerman.

"Is this really necessary?" Michaels asked.

"You tell me," Ackerman said as he ducked down. "I'm not the one who stripped my bank account clean."

"What are you talking about?"

"You stole all my money, you asshole, and I'm going to make you pay if you don't return it."

"I don't know what you're talking about," Michaels said as he looked down at his ball.

"If you draw your detail's attention, I'll fill you full of bullet holes. Consider this mutual assured destruction."

"Okay, okay. Just calm down."

"Is everything all right, Mr. President?" one of the Secret Service agents asked.

"Just fine," Michaels said. "Now stop making me nervous so I can hit this ball."

Ackerman crouched low in the shadows in an effort to remain hidden.

"Just what exactly do you want?" Michaels asked.

"I want my money back," Ackerman said. "I've been doing everything just as you asked and then all of a sudden, my account is zeroed out."

"I can assure you that I had nothing to do with this."

"Are you sure?" Ackerman asked. "I'm not inclined to believe you based on your past history."

"I swear to god that I'm telling you the truth."

Ackerman jammed his gun farther into Michaels' back. "After all I did for you—I can't believe you would treat me like this."

"I don't know what you're talking about, but I can assure you that I've never ordered anyone to take any money from your account. You're one of my most loyal men. Why would I do that?"

"I know you're feeling the heat and you're just trying to tidy up some loose ends. I'm not going to be a loose end or a footnote in your tattered legacy, I can promise you that much."

"Oliver, just calm down."

"No, I won't just calm down. You've got four hours to restore all the money to my account or I'm going public with the truth. And consider this our last working agreement."

"Sir," one of the Secret Service agents called, "are you sure you're all right?"

"Never better," Michaels said as he glanced up at the man and then back down at his ball.

Michaels looked over his shoulder. Ackerman had retreated into the woods and was nowhere to be seen.

Michaels swung hard and topped the ball. He watched it roll a few feet before coming to rest on a root.

"Son of a bitch," Michaels muttered.

And he wasn't talking about his muffed shot.

CHAPTER 26

AFTER HIS MORNING GOLF OUTING, President Michaels settled into a chair in the library at his Camp David cottage and cracked open the latest memoir to rocket up all the bestselling charts. "Common Valor" was a book about by a man named John Sellers, an assassin in the Marines who ditched the military after eight years to go start schools for girls in Afghanistan. Michaels flipped the pages, rolling his eyes at Sellers' depiction of military life as well as his empathy toward the plight of the Afghanis.

More like "Common Bullshit" if you ask me.

Michaels slammed the book shut and tossed it on the coffee table in front of him. He sunk in his chair and stared out at the vivid array of fall colors on display outside. The shuffling of feet in the hallway arrested his attention, and he sat up and looked to see who was there.

"Still mulling over that decision to go for it on

fourteen instead of laying up in front of the water?" David Kriegel asked.

"If I had to do it over again, I'd still go for it," Michaels said. "You know I live my life without regret."

Kriegel took a deep breath and exhaled slowly as he eased into a chair next to Michaels.

"You might want to reconsider that statement," Kriegel said.

"What are you talking about?"

"I'm talking about the hell you're about to go through."

Michaels furrowed his brow. "I'm lost here, David. Are you referring to something that I should know about?"

"The U.S. attorney general is here to speak with you—and I don't think you're going to like what he has to say."

Michaels looked toward the doorway and saw Thomas Preston standing solemnly with his briefcase in hand.

"What are *you* doing here?" Michaels asked.

Kriegel stood up and strode toward the exit. "I'll leave you two alone to discuss things."

Preston stepped inside and pulled the door shut behind him. After setting his briefcase down on the coffee table, Preston occupied the seat Kriegel had been sitting in. For nearly the last four years, Preston had been cleaning house as it pertained to all the corruption in Washington. Bankers, lobbyists, senators, federal judges—no one was beyond Preston's reach. And while the purge had been painful at times for Michaels, he chalked up the loss of friends and allies to the cost of doing business. He concluded that if all these people who claimed to be his friend were skirting the rules and backstabbing confidantes, it would only be a matter of time before they did the same thing to him. Preston had done exactly what Michaels wanted: Washington was no longer a network consisting solely of crooked individuals sticking their fingers in the collective pie. A few miscreants still remained in the shadows, but given enough time, Preston would eventually flush them out or simply shut them down.

"Who is it this time?" Michaels asked.

Preston opened his briefcase and retrieved a file folder.

"I need you to read this," Preston said.

"No problem," Michaels said as he tossed it onto the end table next to his seat.

"Now," Preston ordered.

"Is this really necessary?"

"I'd rather you hear it from me than on the news."

Michaels cocked his head and squinted as he stared at Preston. "Why don't you tell me what this is all about first?"

Preston didn't flinch. "Read it."

Michaels reached for the files and started reading. After reading the first page, he flipped through the document, barely stopping long enough on each page to read more than a sentence or two.

"What's this?" Michaels said, holding the pages up to Preston. "Another partisan hit job? Who even believes this stuff anymore?"

Preston leaned forward and retrieved his laptop from the briefcase. Opening up his computer, he inserted a flash drive into one of the side ports and waited. He clicked on a certain file and placed the laptop on Michaels' desk.

"Have a seat at your desk and watch this," Preston said, waiting for Michaels to sit down before pressing play.

The video began to play. Within the first 30 seconds, Michaels' face turned pale.

"Seen enough?" Preston asked.

Michaels set his jaw and narrowed his eyes. "Who the hell do you think you are?" he asked, pounding his desk.

Noah Young walked into the room and cleared his throat.

"He's Thomas Preston, the U.S. attorney general," Young said. "The one you appointed to clean up all this mess in Washington. Or have you forgotten so soon?"

Big Earv and another Secret Service agent stepped into the room and shut the door behind them.

"Look, can we just talk about this?" Michaels said. He cut his eyes over at the agents. "*Alone?*"

"I'm afraid they need to stick around," Preston said. "Protocol. You understand, right?"

"I'm the president of the United States of America, damn it," Michaels bellowed. "And I want to talk about this without a pair of agents in the room."

Preston nodded at the men and they stepped outside and pulled the door shut.

"Now, please, state your case, Mr. President," Preston said. "I want to hear your explanation for all of this."

"This is entrapment, and you know it," Michaels said. "My lawyers will beat this accusation silly—and you can bet your ass that you'll be relieved of your duties post haste."

"Not when you don't have the power to fire me," Preston said.

"What the hell do you mean? I can do anything I want, I'm the—"

"We know, Conrad," Young said, cutting off his boss. "You're the president of the United States of America. The sad thing is you haven't been acting like it. More to the point, you've been subverting this great country."

"Better to control the threat than let it sneak up on you," Michaels said. "Besides, we now know exactly where Al Hasib is, thanks to my plan."

"Is that so?" Young asked.

"Yes, and I'll prove it to you," Michaels said.

Young slipped a piece of paper on the desk in front of Michaels.

"Is this what you're looking for? Coordinates from the tracking devices?"

Brow furrowed, Michaels looked up at Young. "How did you get—"

"Never mind that. Want me to log into the DOD satellite system and punch in these coordinates?"

"Yes, Noah. Do it right now and show the soon-to-be ex-Attorney General Thomas Preston that I'm more genius than anyone gives me credit for."

"If you insist," Young said before sliding into the chair vacated by Michaels.

Young hammered away on the keyboard until the satellite images came up on the screen.

"Please read the coordinates aloud for me," Young said.

Michaels picked up the piece of paper and followed Young's instructions. After a series of keystrokes, Young stood up and held his hand out toward the computer.

"Please, have a look," he said.

Michaels sat down and zoomed in on the location flagged on the screen.

"Are you sure that's the right location?"

"Sure as I am standing here," Young said.

"But there's nothing there—it's just sand."

"Welcome to the Omani desert, home to thousands of species that can survive with little to no water. And now also home to your tracking device."

"How'd they figure that out? I swear they didn't know about the tracker. Only one person knew about it."

Preston hovered near the desk with his arms crossed. "Was that one person named Oliver Ackerman?"

"Oliver who?"

"Don't even play that game with us," Young said. "You know who he is."

Michaels paused for a moment and looked pensively out the window. He felt the walls closing in around him as the people who held positions of power had encircled him. They didn't appreciate what he was trying to do, especially during an election year.

"The people need to know that there are threats and—"

"Threats you're creating," Young said. "When you keep giving weapons to renegade terrorist leaders who have no conscience, they're going to do unconscionable things with them. How do you not understand this?"

"How do you not understand the limitations of power in this country? We need to annihilate Al Hasib and other groups. But we can't do that under the status quo. Once the people understand the threat, they will give us the power we need to wipe them out."

"That sounds like political posturing to me," Preston said. "And it's not going to fly—not in the court of public opinion or in a congressional hearing. It doesn't matter how many allies you might have on Capitol Hill, they're all going to desert you once this gets out."

A knock on the door interrupted them. Young opened it to find one of Preston's assistants standing solemnly just outside.

"Thomas," Young said, gesturing toward the aide.

Preston strode across the room and asked what was the reason for the intrusion, demanding to know why it couldn't wait.

"It's pertinent, sir," the man said as he handed a cell phone to Preston.

After a few seconds, Preston's jaw dropped. He returned to the desk and handed the phone to Michaels.

"I'm afraid all your bargaining power is now gone, thanks to one Oliver Ackerman," Preston said, showing the phone to Michaels.

Michaels received the device and pressed play. A video of Michaels and Oliver Ackerman seated in what appeared to be something like a CIA black site interview room. The images appeared to come from a camera located in the upper corner of the room.

"What exactly do you want me to do, Mr. President?" Ackerman asked.

"Exactly what I said," Michaels fired back.

"Which is . . ."

"Do I have to spell everything out for you? I want you to set up an arms deal with Al Hasib."

"Sir, with all due respect, are you sure that's a wise idea?"

Michaels put his hand around the back of Oliver's neck and chuckled. *"I know it seems counterintuitive, but there is a method to all this madness."*

"You mind spelling that out for me because I'm lost here."

"Turn it off," Michaels said, turning and looking outside, where he noticed a flurry of activity among the agents. "I'm done with this."

"You weren't very careful, sir," Preston said. "And now the whole world knows about your treasonous act."

"This will never stand up in a court of law," Michaels said.

Preston walked over to the door and opened it. He motioned for the Secret Service agents to enter the room.

"Handcuff him," Preston ordered as he pointed at Michaels.

"What for?" Michaels said. "You have to give a reason for detaining me. It's the law."

Preston sighed as the agents handcuffed Michaels to the arm of his chair. "The last thing you need to be doing is lecturing me about the law. Now, would you like to call your attorney?"

Nostrils flaring, Michaels glared at Preston. "I need you to order these men to release me from custody right now."

Preston shook his head. "Not happening, sir."

"I'm the president, you asshole."

Young smiled. "Not anymore you aren't. Consider yourself relieved of duty."

Michaels jerked at his restraints. "I swear to God, I'm going to kill you, Noah."

Young and the two agents exited the room without another word, leaving Michaels alone with Preston.

Preston eased into the seat on the other side of the desk. He clasped his hands, resting his elbows on the arms of his chair.

"Let's get to the point. I know how much you hate being embarrassed, Conrad. Your legacy? *Poof.* Gone. It's a shame too because you actually made some progress that benefitted all Americans."

"What do you want?"

"I don't want anything, but I am offering you a way out, a way to avoid becoming a stain on the president's office."

"And what makes you think I'm going down for all this? I have really good lawyers, you know."

"No one is going to want your case," Preston said. "You can fight it, but you'll go down. And you sure as hell won't get re-elected next month. October surprise? That'd be a breeze compared to what's about to happen to your poll numbers. Your campaign will become ground zero."

"Suppose you're right about all this. What can you possibly do to ensure that my legacy remains intact?"

Preston picked up his briefcase and opened it. He removed a rope and a knife and placed them on the desk in front of Michaels.

"This is your decision now," Preston said. "You can control how you go. And I promise to make sure that this other information never sees the light of day after the public is told that you died tragically from a sudden embolism in your heart."

"Is this some kind of joke?" Michaels asked.

"Let's just see what the pundits are saying."

Preston grabbed the remote from the edge of the desk and turned on the television. For the next ten minutes, Michaels watched in silence as every political talking head eviscerated him for the leaked video. No one was willing to defend him, much less call for everyone to wait until all the facts came out. The writing was on the wall—his career was over. And Preston offered him what amounted to a virtual pardon, albeit one that ended in death.

"Okay," Michaels said. "I'll accept your offer as long as you promise to keep your word. Defend me on this and make up a plausible cover story. Don't let them tarnish what I've done over a single mistake."

"You have my word," Preston said. "Now, what'll it be?"

Michaels nodded toward the knife.

"It'll be quick and painless as far as suicides go—and easier to cover up."

Preston gathered all his items, including his laptop and the rope, and placed them into his briefcase. He slipped the thumb drive into his coat pocket and strode toward the door.

Stopping at the door, he turned back to Michaels and threw him the keys to the handcuffs.

"You've got half an hour," Preston said.

Michaels watched the door shut before he started to unlock himself. He rubbed his wrists and then stared down at the knife. Picking it up, he fingered the blade before he pricked his thumb. He watched a drop of blood bead up before dripping onto the desk.

He closed his eyes and put the knife against his wrist.

Here goes nothing.

CHAPTER 27

HAWK KEPT HIS FOOT on the gas as he wound along the two-lane roads leading to Camp David. For too long, President Michaels had played games with Hawk, placing him on terrorist watch and most-wanted lists. Hawk had grown tired of living with his head on a swivel. But even more importantly, he'd grown tired of serving under a president who was a bigger threat to the country than the tough-talking terrorists oceans away from U.S. soil.

Hawk called Big Earv, his longtime friend and Secret Service agent, to find out if there was anything he should know about Michaels' visit to the presidential retreat.

"Big Earv, where are you?" Hawk asked once his friend answered.

"I'm at Camp David with the president."

"Think you can get me a private meeting with him, one that's totally off the books?"

Big Earv sighed. "I'm not sure that's a good idea, Hawk. I just went off duty, but there's some crazy stuff going on up here right now."

"Such as?"

"The VP and the attorney general both just arrived a few hours ago. They met with Michaels in the library and talked for a while. I was posted outside on duty and told not to let anyone inside. After the VP and attorney general exited, they told me not to let Michaels out. My shift ended a few minutes ago, but Michaels was still sequestered in there."

"Alex was right."

"Right about what? She said she had something brewing that was going to get Michaels in hot water and end him through legal channels."

"Well, she might be right but nobody knows what's going on. We haven't been told anything other than our supervisor telling us to protect the president but that he wasn't in charge anymore."

"What could that mean?"

"I don't know. Something is happening, something big. But nobody is talking about it."

"You didn't hear anything while you were standing at your post outside his library?" Hawk asked.

"No, at least nothing that I could make sense of. It sounded like they were watching a video. Michaels demanded that we leave the room."

"Thanks for the heads up. I just wanted to let you know that I'll be up there soon."

"I don't know if that's a good idea, Hawk. This place is on high alert. I've never seen anything like it. If someone dropped a bomb on this place right now, it'd be chaos in Washington."

"Don't worry. I'll be careful."

Hawk hung up and checked his GPS. He was only ten minutes away.

CHAPTER 28

MICHAELS WATCHED THE BLOOD trickle down his wrist before changing his mind. *I'm not a quitter—never have been, never will be.* He stopped cutting before he reached any substantial arteries and grabbed a blanket from a chair in the corner of the room. Ripping a swatch off, he wrapped it around his wrist until the bleeding stopped.

He glanced at the clock. There were five minutes remaining before Thomas Preston returned to the room and expected to find his president dead. But Michaels had worked too hard to go down without a fight.

I'm the president, damn it. I should be able to do what I want.

Michaels mulled over his options, which weren't as numerous as he hoped for. Since he'd ruled out suicide, he could fight everything in court, where his chances were conservatively 60-40 that he'd win. Despite any accusations, most Americans still admired anyone who won the presidency, even if they hated the man. Or he could make a run for it and try to disappear. The odds of just blending in weren't in his favor. Or he could spin the whole thing and make Noah Young take the fall. It'd be risky, but it could be done. Michaels put those odds at 50-50.

But none of that would matter if he didn't figure out a way to escape Preston's iron fist. Michaels contemplated how he would handle the return of the attorney general to his library. Would it be a violent surprise attack? An attempt to appeal to Preston's humanity? Maybe even a bribe would work?

Michaels concluded all those would have to wait. He needed Preston's discovery to be dramatic.

As the clock wound down, Michaels braced himself and rehearsed exactly what he'd say.

Tick, tick, tick.

The seconds passed by slowly. Michaels shifted in his chair and spun it around so that his back was to the door.

At exactly thirty minutes after Preston had left, he re-entered the room. He shut the door behind him after instructing the two Secret Service agents on guard to remain outside in case he needed them.

The floorboards creaked as he crept across the room to inspect the scene of a dead president. Michaels sat motionless, his left hand dangling at his side.

"What the—"

Preston froze when he looked at the floor and didn't see much blood. Without warning, Michaels reached up and grabbed Preston's hand.

"I'm disappointed in you," Preston said.

"Not half as much as I am in you," Michaels said through clenched teeth. "I trusted you. I gave you a chance when no one else would. And *this* is the thanks I get?"

Preston wrestled his arm away from Michaels and took a step back.

"You're out of your mind," Preston said. "I wanted to protect you, but I can't now if you try to walk outside those doors."

"You wanted to protect me? You? Protect me? By what—giving me a knife so I would kill myself? From where I sit, it appears that you wanted to save yourself the headache of prosecuting a sitting president. Well, you're not getting off that easily."

"The whole world is going to see what's on that thumb drive," Preston said. "Is that really what you want? The American people are going to see you betraying your country, the one they elected you to protect."

"It'll never stand up in court and you know it," Michaels said. "That's why you've staged this whole charade. You and that stooge, Noah Young, have no idea what you're up against."

Preston rubbed his face with his hands before addressing Michaels.

"You really think you know how this is all going to go down? I've got news for you, *Mr. President.* I have friends in high places as well—and all of them would love to see you go down in flames."

"I demand your resignation right now," Michaels said.

"Really? Good luck with that because I'm not resigning from anything. I'm going to see this through for the good of our country. I tried to do you a favor before, but not anymore. You're going to go down, but it won't be in a blaze of glory. It'll be more like flittering ashes as you and your pathetic legacy drift to the ground."

Michaels narrowed his eyes. "Where did you get that video from? Who sent it to you? Do you even know?"

"Are you challenging its legitimacy? I'll have experts lined up to testify that it's your voice, not to mention Pentagon generals who loathe your leadership and will be frothing at the mouth to verify all your illegal activities."

"Did someone send this to you?" Michaels asked.

"What does that have to do with anything?"

"Do you have a backup copy, or did you come straight here with this?"

"What?"

Before Preston could get another word out, Michaels recoiled before driving his knife into the attorney general's hand and pinning it to the desk.

Preston let out a visceral scream before Michaels snatched the thumb drive out of Preston's other hand.

"You'll never get away with this," Preston said.

Michaels didn't look back, storming through the door and racing down the hallway. He heard Preston scream for the Secret Service agents to arrest the president, but it was too late. Michaels had already left the house and raced into the wooded area surrounding the Camp David cottage.

Serves the bastard right.

Michaels glanced to his left and right. He didn't see a soul as he ventured into the forest.

CHAPTER 29

HAWK TOOK A PRONE POSITION about 200 meters away from the Camp David cottage. Wearing camouflage and nestled against the ground, he pulled out his binoculars and peered through them at the activity inside. He felt as if he'd entered into a life of voyeurism, switching back and forth between the rooms. Despite pushing the twinge of guilt down, he couldn't deny that *something* was happening, the kind of something that Big Earv had referenced in describing the scene.

Hawk bounced back and forth between the various rooms in the house, catching glimpses of the people inside as they moved around. Whatever was taking place, Hawk concluded that Big Earv was right—the peaceful status quo had been long since abandoned. Secret Service agents darted around the house while Thomas Preston appeared to be in anguish.

"What the hell?" Hawk muttered to himself as he watched Preston contort his face but remain in the library.

Hawk's field of vision drifted downward until he could see the full picture and caught the source of Preston's anguish. A knife appeared to be buried in the back of Preston's hand.

Preston continued screaming and crying for help.

Hawk whipped the binoculars over to the den, which had an exit leading to the back porch. Michaels eased outside and said something to the agent posted by the door. The agent dashed inside, leaving Michaels alone outside. As Hawk watched, Michaels checked over his shoulder once more and surveyed the wooded area behind the house before taking off and sprinting toward the forest.

Does he think he's going to disappear?

Hawk smiled as he refocused his binoculars and followed Michaels' pathway into the woods. Michaels was headed straight for Hawk.

While Hawk followed Michaels, a Secret Service agent poked his head outside and called out.

"Mr. President? Mr. President? Are you outside?" the agent asked.

Michaels didn't even turn around, continuing to beat a path deep into the forest.

Hawk watched the agent squint as he peered into

dense vegetation behind the house before shrugging and returning inside.

After another fifteen seconds, Michaels neared Hawk's position.

* * *

MICHAELS PAUSED TO CATCH his breath. Bending over with his hands resting on his knees, he closed his eyes and tried to gather his thoughts. Left alone with the knife in his library, Michaels had time to formulate a plan, though a hasty one. Before he set it in motion, he realized it was far from perfect and would need everything to fall his way in order to survive the impending scandal. But it was better than slashing his wrist.

Michaels stood upright and scanned the woods, deciding on his next path. Before he took off running, his phone rang. Michaels pulled it out to inspect it. Anxious to answer the call, he tapped the screen and said hello.

"How'd you get this number? I never give it out," Michaels said with a scowl.

"Seriously? That's the first question you ask me," a man said. Hawk recognized the voice almost immediately. It was Oliver Ackerman.

Michaels spoke in a whisper. "What do you want?"

"I think I already made that clear earlier. I want all my money back."

"I don't know what you're talking about," Michaels said. "I never took your money."

"How come my account is empty then?"

"Maybe there was a computer glitch."

"I called the bank. There's nothing in there. And there's only one person who knew about that account."

Michaels sighed. "Apparently not—because I had nothing to do with it, unless your bank is taking you for a ride. I've heard those financial institutions in the Caribbean aren't always on the up and up."

"I called the bank and they traced the withdrawal back to your people."

"Like I said, must've been a mistake. Or perhaps there's some rogue staffer in my office doing unscrupulous things with your account. But I don't have time to hash this over."

"Well, you're going to make time to put everything back as it should be or else I'm going to release proof of who the real President Conrad Michaels is."

Michaels looked around as he spoke. "Then you'd never get your money—and I'd deny everything. Meanwhile, you'd spend the rest of your life in jail."

"I'm sure you're familiar with the acronym MAD—mutually assured destruction."

Michaels chuckled. "If you make a play like that, it'll be SAD—self-assured destruction—because I sure as hell won't go down for anything you've done over there. And before you get any ideas, just remember how that whole Wikileaks scandal turned out. Nobody believes a damn thing they say anymore."

"Put the money back in the account and this all goes away," Ackerman said. "We'll go our separate ways and never speak of this day again. Otherwise, you'll never forget it and rue your stubbornness until the moment you breathe your last breath."

"You'll never see a dime from me again. Burn in hell, Ollie," Michaels said before he hung up.

He shoved his phone into his pocket and felt the thumb drive. Escaping so he could regroup was a high priority, but not as important as destroying the video that could actually ruin his presidency, not to mention his entire legacy.

Michaels looked around for an appropriate spot and identified a location near the base of a tree that was shrouded by a large fern. The spot was off the beaten path and wouldn't likely be discovered by even the most observant searchers. Michaels knelt down next to the tree and dug down a foot before hitting some rocks and deciding the hole was deep enough. Dropping the flash drive into the hole, he carefully covered it back up and dropped a thick coat of pine straw on top.

If they ever do find that, it'll be too late.

Michaels dusted his hands off and identified the path he'd chosen earlier. Pausing only to look behind him and noticing no one was searching for him yet, he blasted into the woods.

* * *

HAWK WATCHED AS MICHAELS tore through the forest, his head down and feet sure. Michaels leapt over a fallen pine and pumped his arms as he moved. For a moment, Hawk was mesmerized that Michaels hadn't lost more than a step from his acclaimed career as a track star in college. Michaels pumped his arms and breathed heavily.

But with his head down, Michaels never saw Hawk—or his locked arm. Catching Michaels right in the throat, Hawk smiled wryly as the president went airborne and landed on his back.

Michaels hit the ground with a thud, followed almost immediately by a moan.

"Nice of you to stop by, Conrad. Seems like we always seem to meet when you're in desperate need of some help."

Michaels groaned before letting out a string of expletives directed at Hawk.

"I'm not sure denigrating me is the best approach when I'm the only person who can give you a hand."

Wide-eyed, Michaels looked up at Hawk.

"You'll help me?"

Hawk shook his head. "Not a chance. Today is when it all ends. You, me, the American people—we all need to come to a better understanding about who you really are and what you're really doing during your presidency."

"Think you can stop me?" Michaels jeered.

Hawk reached for his gun tucked in the back of his belt.

"Settle down," a man said a few meters downhill from Hawk and Michaels' position.

"Big Earv," Hawk said. "About time you arrived."

"Put the gun down, Hawk," Big Earv said. "You don't wanna do this. This isn't you."

Hawk cocked his head and frowned. "Isn't me? What are you talking about? This is all I do. I take out the trash. And this sack here has a stench that's overwhelming."

"There are better ways to handle this."

"Name one."

Michaels sat up. "You let me go and I'll appoint you to some position in the Pentagon."

"Shut up," Hawk said. "You couldn't pay me all the money in the world to sit behind a desk and kiss bureaucratic ass all day long. Besides, my character isn't up for sale."

"There are legal channels to take him down," Big Earv said, glancing at Michaels.

"So my own Secret Service agents aren't even on my side?" Michaels said. "Unbelievable."

"Is that really so hard to believe?" Hawk asked. "You've treated people as if they were your slaves doing your bidding for a long time. It's how you got to the top, but it's going to cost you everything now."

"The attorney general has a plan," Big Earv said. "He briefed us before sending us out to look for Michaels—and he said the most important thing is to bring him back alive."

"That's a change," Michaels grumbled. "He was trying to get me to kill myself not even an hour ago."

"Perhaps you shouldn't have pinned his hand to a desk with a knife," Hawk said.

"How'd you see that?" Michaels asked.

Big Earv sighed. "Look, I'd love to discuss all the details leading up to this moment with both of you— and I'm sure we will at some point—but I need to get the president back to the cottage."

"You really think that's the best idea?" Hawk asked. "I think there's another way we can handle all this."

Michaels immediately began to hyperventilate.

"Would you simmer down?" Hawk said. "Your opinion doesn't really matter at this point."

"My chest," Michaels said. "Look on my chest. There's a red dot on it."

Hawk and Big Earv both inspected the red point that danced around the center of Michaels' chest.

"It's over, Conrad," Ackerman said as he lumbered toward them, his gun still trained on Michaels. "Let's finish this now."

Big Earv pulled his gun out and aimed it at Ackerman.

"Drop the weapon," Big Earv said. "Whatever beef you have with Michaels, get in line. And just know that it isn't worth it."

Ackerman laughed. "You want me to have mercy on this lowlife con artist? I'm doing the American people a favor by taking him off the ticket next month."

Michael glared at Ackerman. "Just do it already, but don't try to take some sanctimonious position based on what you do. You're lower than low."

"You do nothing but use and abuse everyone around you," Ackerman said. "You deal in the currency of terror while proclaiming to be the one who will protect us all against the threats of our enemies, enemies you helped create."

"And you're the one who carries out those orders," Michaels said. "you seeing the disconnect here, Ollie?"

"The honesty from both of you is refreshing," Hawk said. "And while I'd prefer to see both of you die right here and now, Big Earv has spoken. Now put your gun down, Ackerman."

250 | R.J. PATTERSON

"Well, if *Chuck Pearl* tells me to do something, then I better do it. Ain't that right, Brady Hawk?" Ackerman said with a sneer.

"I heard you were amused at making me stick with my legend," Hawk said, "but I doubt you were amused at the mess I made of your scheduled delivery to Al Hasib. That's probably what drove you here, isn't it? You're seeking sanctuary after the botched deal and Al Hasib made you public enemy number one. Tell me I'm wrong."

"Shut up," Ackerman said. "I have half a mind to put a bullet in you first."

"How about you and I both save all the bullets in our guns," Big Earv said. "Now, drop your weapon before I handle your defiance in a way that I'm sure you won't enjoy."

"Why? So you can put me behind bars next to this piece of shit?" Ackerman said, gesturing toward Michaels.

"You and I both know I'm not going to prison," Michaels said as a mocking grin spread across his face.

Ackerman didn't hesitate. He pulled the trigger and fired two shots in Michaels' center mass. Ackerman turned to take aim at Hawk before collapsing to the ground. Hawk and Big Earv each put a couple of bullets in Ackerman. He was dead before he hit the dirt.

"What's going on over there?" called another Secret Service agent through the woods.

"The president has been hit," Big Earv said into his com. "I repeat, the president has been hit. I'm on site and handling it."

He turned to Hawk. "You better get lost—and fast. You don't need to answer for any of this or find yourself in the middle of any congressional hearings."

"Thanks, Big Earv. I owe you."

"No, you don't. Now get lost before you'll need more than a favor to escape prison."

Hawk nodded and hustled up the hill, disappearing deep into the forest enveloping Camp David. He ran until his sides hurt before falling to his knees in exhaustion. After all that had just transpired, he needed some kind of emotional release, but he dared not scream in case he drew the attention of some other Secret Service agents. And Hawk couldn't conjure up a tear if his life depended upon it. He refused to shed anything for Michaels.

I can't believe he's gone.

Hawk snapped to his feet when he heard helicopters hovering overhead. After racing a few meters through the woods, he stopped when he noticed that the helicopter was setting down in a clearing less than a hundred meters away.

Checking over his shoulder once more, he

dashed in the opposite direction of his car. He glanced at the field and watched as a dozen soldiers stormed from the chopper and fanned out.

Hawk scrambled up a short hill before he skidded to a stop and struggled to maintain his balance. He'd nearly plummeted into a rocky ravine some fifty meters below. After he regained his composure, he looked back at the clearing where the soldiers had come from. Two men dressed in Army combat fatigues hustled toward Hawk, both guns trained on him.

"Don't make this any harder than it has to be," one of the soldiers said.

Hawk raised his hands in surrender.

"Someone wants to speak with you," the other soldier said.

He took Hawk's hands and zip tied them behind his back.

CHAPTER 30

Washington, D.C.

HAWK CLIMBED ABOARD the troop transport helicopter and sat down against the wall. He buckled in and took the headset offered to him by one of the soldiers who apprehended him. Adjusting the earpiece, Hawk looked up and stared directly across the chopper at a man dressed in a suit and tie.

"Mr. Vice President," Hawk said.

A smile spread across Noah Young's face. "I heard you were in the neighborhood and thought I'd give you a lift," he said into the microphone on his headset.

"Next time, can you tell your men to give me a heads up?" Hawk said. "I was plotting how I could jump out of this bird without breaking my ankles so I could escape."

Young chuckled. "We haven't lifted off yet, so there's still time if you want to test your theory."

Hawk shook his head. "So, what's this all about, really?"

"Well, I'm headed back to Washington now to be installed as the new president."

"Why not take Air Force One instead of this old clunker?"

"Too soon and too raw, though I did consider it."

"You moved really quickly on this," Hawk said.

"The plan for me to take over was already in motion. Thomas Preston was satisfied that he had enough on Michaels to put him away for life for committing treason along with a hefty list of other crimes. But now that he's dead, I don't have to waste this last month on trying to extricate myself from a needless trial."

"Who else knows about this?" Hawk asked.

"Just a handful of the cabinet—and we intend to keep it that way."

Hawk scowled. "You're not going to tell the truth about what Michaels was doing?"

"Maybe someday, but not today. A scandal like this will just tear the country apart even more than it already is. It's just not necessary."

"So, what's the official narrative going to be?"

"One of Michaels' ex-military pals had a long-standing grudge with the president. Ackerman snuck onto the Camp David property using his army training and shot Michaels, who lied to a Secret Service agent to meet the friend. The Secret Service agent gunned down the killer before he shot anyone else."

"So, Big Earv is a hero?"

"He soon will be."

"Good. If anyone deserves it, he does. But he won't like having to cop to that story."

"He doesn't have a choice, thanks to you."

"What do you mean?" Hawk asked.

"He knew you might be sneaking onto the property and told no one. But one of the other agents picked up his phone call and told us about it. We held that card up our sleeve in the event that something like this happened."

"You're blackmailing him to make him the hero?"

"That's one way of looking at it. I'd rather just say it's how we're ensuring that he sticks to the story. It'll be much less of a headache if he repeats the rehearsed version of the events we're going to give him."

"Fair enough."

"But you didn't pick me up and take me back to Washington just to discuss all this, now did you?"

Young shook his head. "I want to talk about your future and the future of Firestorm."

"No disrespect, sir, but how can you be doing that when you're only going to be in power for the next few weeks?"

"I have plans of sticking around much longer."

"You're going to be on the ticket next month?"

"That's the plan. The party will hold an emergency meeting tonight to decide who will replace Michaels in the general election next month. And I have an overwhelming amount of support."

"And you think you'll be able to forge a new identity apart from Michaels' coattails in that short amount of time?" Hawk asked.

"I'll have some of the best political strategists in the world to help me. So, if anyone can do it, they can."

Hawk nodded. "You'll have my vote."

"I was hoping for more than that," Young said. "I was hoping to have your commitment—a vow to reignite Firestorm with full support from this office and more resources."

"I'm open to considering it, depending on what Blunt and Alex say. But why the urgency?"

Young sighed and shook his head. "We got word that Al Hasib is planning another attack. And if they succeed, their numbers are only going to swell. We need a win by taking out Karif Fazil and delivering a blow to their operation. And you're the one person we trust to pull it off."

"I'm honored, sir. But like I mentioned earlier, Firestorm is not just me. We're a team. If Alex and

Blunt are in, you can count on me. We're a package deal."

"Very well then. That's all I can ask for at the moment. I trust you'll all choose to return. There's still some unfinished business you have to do."

"I'll consider it and let you know as soon as possible," Hawk said. "I appreciate your commitment to Firestorm. It's vital to our country's security, and I'm proud to be a part of such a talented group of people."

Young nodded knowingly. They rode in silence the rest of the trip, while Hawk was lost in his thoughts.

* * *

THREE DAYS LATER, Hawk met Alex and Blunt at the airport. Clutching a bouquet of flowers, Hawk wasted no time in thrusting them into Alex's hands once she exited the secure area.

"Hawk!" she said. "What ever did I do to deserve this?"

"Please don't make me come up with something mushy," Hawk said. "That's not my style."

Out of the corner of his eye, Hawk caught Blunt staring.

"What? Are you jealous I didn't bring *you* any flowers?"

Blunt chuckled. "You know by now that I only give flowers when I want to bug someone, right?"

Hawk gave Alex a long hug and then took her by the shoulders before looking her in the eyes. "You know I'd never do that to you, don't you? But the senator on the other hand . . ."

Hawks' words trailed off as he shot a sly grin at Blunt.

"I need to get a drink—and we need to discuss the future of this team," Blunt said as he snatched his carryon bag and wheeled it behind him. He walked toward the exit with authority and purpose.

"What happened to your cane?" Hawk asked Blunt.

"I don't need a cane," Blunt said.

"It was a prop?"

"Sometimes," Blunt said. "Other times, it was a certified weapon."

"Now that that's settled, I don't need a drink to answer the question that we all need to answer right now," Hawk said. "Is everybody still in for Firestorm?"

"Sure beats working for a bank," Alex said.

"I'll take that as a *yes*," Hawk said. "And what about you, Senator? You still got it in you to keep going until we dismantle these terrorists one by one, starting with Karif Fazil and Al Hasib?"

"Wouldn't want to do anything else," Blunt said.

"In that case, let's go get some drinks—and celebrate," Alex said.

"Wait a minute," Hawk said. "We haven't *all* committed just yet."

Alex sighed and hung her head. "I can't believe that it's been so long I almost forgot about my half brother."

"It's okay," Hawk said. "Given the circumstances, it's understandable. But I want to know what's up with Samuels."

"As we all do," Blunt said.

"Give me just a moment," Hawk said.

Hawk slipped away from his two colleagues and dialed Young's number.

"Do you have an answer for me?" Young asked.

"Almost," Hawk said.

"What's the holdup?"

"Shane Samuels," Hawk said. "What happened to him and where is he?"

"I've been meaning to talk to you about him."

"Please explain. And no beating around the bush."

"The long and the short of it is that Samuels isn't who you think he is."

Hawk furrowed his brow. "What do you mean? Who is he?"

"I can't talk about this right now, but let me assure you that he never really was part of your team, if you catch my drift."

"He was a mole?"

"More or less. But we can discuss this at length at a later date. The Firestorm team deserves an explanation, and it's going to take a while to catch you up to speed."

"In that case, I guess I'm calling to let you know that we're in," Hawk said.

"Excellent. I'll be in touch about setting you up with new headquarters for Blunt and Alex as well as getting you going on your first mission. We don't have much time to waste."

Hawk hung up and jammed his hands into his coat pocket. He took a deep breath and strode back toward Blunt and Alex. Despite the mystery surrounding Samuels, Hawk hadn't felt so free in years. Michaels was gone. The Chamber was decimated. Only Al Hasib remained, though it too had suffered tremendous setbacks in recent years.

And Hawk couldn't wait to finish the job.

THE END

ACKNOWLEDGMENTS

I am grateful to so many people who have helped with the creation of this project and the entire Brady Hawk series.

Krystal Wade has been a fantastic help in handling the editing of this book, and Dwight Kuhlman has produced another great audio version for your listening pleasure.

I would also like to thank my advance reader team for all their input in improving this book along with all the other readers who have enthusiastically embraced the story of Brady Hawk. Stay tuned ... there's more Brady Hawk coming soon.

ABOUT THE AUTHOR

R.J. PATTERSON is an award-winning writer living in southeastern Idaho. He first began his illustrious writing career as a sports journalist, recording his exploits on the soccer fields in England as a young boy. Then when his father told him that people would pay him to watch sports if he would write about what he saw, he went all in. He landed his first writing job at age 15 as a sports writer for a daily newspaper in Orangeburg, S.C. He later attended earned a degree in newspaper journalism from the University of Georgia, where he took a job covering high school sports for the award-winning *Athens Banner-Herald* and *Daily News*.

He later became the sports editor of *The Valdosta Daily Times* before working in the magazine world as an editor and freelance journalist. He has won numerous writing awards, including a national award for his investigative reporting on a sordid tale surrounding an NCAA investigation over the University of Georgia football program.

R.J. enjoys the great outdoors of the Northwest while living there with his wife and four children. He still follows sports closely. He also loves connecting with readers and would love to hear from you. To stay updated about future projects, connect with him over Facebook or on the interwebs at www.RJPbooks.com and sign up for his newsletter to get deals and updates.

Made in the USA
Middletown, DE
18 August 2021